* * *

Their lips met with an unexpected spark.

She didn't pull away. The old Emma would have. In her mask, she was someone else.

She wrapped her arms around his neck, her lips clinging to his as he probed and explored her with his tongue. It was deliciously naughty. In that moment, Emma wanted it more than anything else in her entire life.

"Come with me," he whispered.

Emma knew what he was offering and every inch of her body urged her to take him up on it. She'd never done anything like this. Ever. And yet there was something about her hero that insisted she go with him.

So she did.

Little Secrets: Secretly Pregnant

ANDREA LAURENCE

First published in Great Britain 2017
By Mills & Boon, an imprint of HarperCollins*Publishers*
1 London Bridge Street, London, SE1 9GF

Large Print edition 2017

© 2017 Andrea Laurence

ISBN: 978-0-263-07220-4

MIX
Paper from
responsible sources
FSC™ C007454

Printed and bound in Great Britain
by CPI Group (UK) Ltd, Croydon, CR0 4YY

Andrea Laurence is an award-winning author of contemporary romances filled with seduction and sass. She has been a lover of reading and writing stories since she was young. A dedicated West Coast girl transplanted into the Deep South, she is thrilled to share her special blend of sensuality and dry, sarcastic humour with readers.

To Dan
Thanks for the inspiration

Prologue

Fat Tuesday

Everyone was dancing and having a good time. Everyone except Emma. That wasn't unusual, though. Emma Dempsey had forgotten how to have fun a long time ago.

After her recent breakup, she was beginning to wonder if something was wrong with her. Her ex, David, had said she was boring both in and out of bed. She made the mistake of telling that to her friend and former sorority sister, Harper Drake, and the next thing she knew, she was at a Mardi Gras party at a loft in Tribeca.

She'd tried. She wore a pretty butterfly mask and a tight skirt, but this just wasn't her cup of tea. Perhaps she should just call a cab and go so she didn't ruin Harper's night. She nibbled absently on a carrot stick as her gaze fell upon a tequila bar that had been set up on the kitchen island beside her. That was always a second option.

Emma knew she had to make a choice. She could either go home and join a local Red Hat Society at the ripe age of twenty-seven or she could take this bull by the horns and have some fun for once.

Feeling brave, she abandoned her plate and moved down the island. There was an assortment of small paper cups, slices of lime, a salt shaker and several bottles of tequila laid out. She prepared a shot and held it there, knowing once she leaped off the cliff, there would be no turning back.

Being with you is like dating my grandma. The memory of David's painful words pushed her over the edge.

Without further hesitation, she licked, drank

and sucked the lime furiously to cover the flavor of the liquor. It burned her throat as it went down, splashing in her stomach and sending a scorching sensation almost immediately through her body that a beer couldn't even come close to.

It tasted absolutely terrible, but within seconds, she could feel a pleasant change. Almost as though her spine had loosened. Slinky. Maybe feline. This wasn't bad at all. With a smile of satisfaction, she poured a second shot as someone else came into the kitchen. A quick glance confirmed her worst fears.

"Hey there, beautiful," a creepy guy in a Batman-like mask said, leaning against the counter.

The compliment fell flat considering 75 percent of her face was covered in an ornate Mardi Gras mask. Emma sighed and slammed back the second shot of tequila without salt or lime. She needed it. She started pouring a third, blatantly ignoring him.

"Would you like to dance? I've got some sweet moves."

She doubted it. "I don't dance, sorry."

Batman frowned. "Well, then wanna blow this

party off for someplace quiet and dark where we can…talk?"

A shudder ran down Emma's spine. Being alone with him was bad enough. Alone in the dark was downright frightening. "No, I'm here with someone. Sorry."

Batman straightened up, his body language projecting the anger his mask hid away. "Who?"

She opened her mouth to answer him when someone came up behind her and set heavy, warm hands on her shoulders. He leaned in, placing a kiss against her cheek, and Batman finally took a step back.

A deep male voice rumbled near her ear. "Hey, baby, sorry I'm late."

Emma fought the urge to pull away from this second, undesired suitor, but the fingers pressing insistently in her shoulders begged for her cooperation. He wasn't putting the moves on her; he was trying to save her from Batman. Relieved, she turned to face the man and moved without hesitation to say hello.

Whoa. He was taller than she expected, a few inches over six foot, but she couldn't look surprised and convince Batman to bugger off. She strained on tiptoe to reach up and kiss the lips that were the only part of his face visible with a gold-and-green Venetian mask obscuring the rest.

The instant their lips touched, the simple greeting turned into something else. The electricity of the kiss nearly knocked her backward, but his firm, yet gentle grip on her arms wouldn't let her fall away. Her senses were instantly overloaded by the scent of soap and a spicy men's cologne, the soft brush of his lips against hers and the heat of his skin.

Emma wasn't sure if it was the tequila or his kiss, but she was suddenly very aware of her body. The nearness of the man made her skin tingle and her breath quicken. She felt her body leaning into him without her consent. It had to be the tequila. No wonder people got into so much trouble with this stuff.

Regaining some of her senses, she pulled away to break the kiss, but he didn't immediately let go. Batman must still be watching. "I've missed you," she said, snuggling suggestively into him.

His arms wrapped around her and hugged her tightly against the solid wall of his chest. He leaned in, breathing the scent of her hair and whispered, "He left, but he's watching us from the other side of the room. Keep it convincing if you don't want him coming back."

Emma nodded and pulled away. She reached up to affectionately rub a bit of lipstick from her white knight's mouth. The gesture was intimate and quite convincing, she was sure. Once away from him, she had a better view. The mask obscured most of his face, so all she could really decipher was his tall, broad build, tightly fitting jeans and his attractive and bright smile.

"Are we doing tequila shots?" he asked.

"I was, but I think I'm done." She'd had just enough to make this scene authentic, but too much more was trouble for sure.

"Don't be a quitter." He poured himself a shot, and then paused only for a moment to smile wickedly before leaning forward and licking a patch of exposed skin just above her cleavage. Emma sucked a ragged, surprised breath into her chest and held it there. She couldn't respond.

Every impulse in her brain was telling her to step back and stop him, but she just stood there, the tequila rendering her mute.

He hesitated, the salt shaker in his hand. His dark blue eyes connected with hers, awaiting her permission. Could she give it? She wanted to. This was what she'd set out for tonight, even if she hadn't known it. Grandmas didn't do body shots with strangers at parties. But the words still escaped her. All she could do was tip her head back to let him sprinkle the salt gently over the swell of her breasts and place the wedge of lime delicately between her lips.

He came closer, shot in hand. Her entire body ached with anticipation as his hot breath hovered over her skin. He licked slowly, taking longer than she ever expected to remove every grain from her chest. Surely Batman wasn't watching that closely. When he tipped the glass back, swallowing the tequila in one sip, she was finally able to release the air she'd held painfully in her lungs. Then he set the cup down.

Emma tensed, not quite sure what to do aside from holding perfectly still as his hand slipped around her neck to cradle her head and tip her mouth up to him. He dipped his head, his lips brushing hers briefly before biting down and sucking the lime juice. A cool, tart stream of it flowed into her own mouth before his teeth tugged the rind away.

When he took a step back, Emma did the same. It had taken everything she had not to moan aloud when he'd touched her this time. The best thing she could do was to get out of this situation before she lost what little control he'd left her with. Never mind that her face had to be flushed with embarrassment and unexpected arousal.

Her hand self-consciously came to her face and brushed the rough, glittery surface of her mask. She'd forgotten he couldn't see her. Even if she was beet red, he wouldn't know it. She was anonymous tonight. Somehow the knowledge made her bolder and she fought her flight reflex to hold her position by the bar.

He picked up her full paper cup from the counter and held it up in a dangerous and silent offer. It was her turn.

A quick glance confirmed that Batman had disappeared and there was no reason to continue with the show. Aside from her not wanting to stop. "He's gone," she said, giving him the opportunity to stop if this was still just a ruse.

"I know," he said, and handed her the salt shaker.

Given that he was wearing a long-sleeved button-down black shirt, the only real option she had was his neck. She stood on her toes, straining in her heels to reach him. Emma leaned in and left a moist trail from the hollow of his throat to just over his Adam's apple, where her tongue ran across the rough stubble that had grown in since his morning shave. She could feel his pulse quicken as she hovered near to him. This time, she noticed his skin smelled more distinctly male. Salty and slightly musky. She couldn't help lingering to take in a deep breath and commit the scent to memory. Her body's reaction to it was almost primal, parts deep inside of her clenching with a building need.

"Here," he offered as she pulled away to apply the salt. He lowered onto his knees and looked up at her with big blue eyes, his hands resting on the swell of her hips.

Emma could hardly see enough of his face to piece together an expression, but his intense gaze urged her on. As he knelt, it almost felt as though he were worshipping at her feet. She liked it.

She tried to focus on doing the shot properly before his skin dried and the salt wouldn't adhere. She didn't want to give away her inexperience with this. She'd never even dreamed of doing anything as blatantly sexual as body shots. She didn't think she had it in her.

She sprinkled the salt on his throat and positioned the lime between his full, soft lips. Nervously gripping the tequila in one hand, Emma leaned in a second time to lick off the salt. She could feel the vibration of a growl in his throat as her tongue slid across his skin. Pulling away, she quickly threw back the drink and placed her hands on each side of his face. Just before she was able to bite into the fruit, he spat out the lime. Emma didn't have time to stop and their lips met with another unexpected spark.

She didn't pull away. The old Emma would have. In her mask, she was someone else.

The second kiss blew the first out of the water. His fingertips dug into the flesh of her hips as he tugged her close against him. She melted against his mouth, slowly slipping down until she, too, was on her knees in the kitchen. The island shielded them from the crowd only feet away. She wrapped her arms around his neck, her lips clinging to his as he probed and explored her with his tongue.

It was deliciously naughty. In that moment, Emma wanted his kiss more than anything else in her entire life.

Just when she'd convinced herself that the kiss might never end, they parted. His quick breath was hot on the skin of her neck as he pressed his cheek against hers and sat there for a moment to recover. Their arms were still tangled around one another, neither grip loosening. There was an intensity in him that excited and frightened her, but she matched it with her own.

"Come with me," he whispered, then stood and offered his hand.

Emma wasn't ignorant. She knew what he was offering and every inch of her body urged her to take him up on it. She'd never done anything like this. Ever. And yet there was something about her hero that insisted she go with him.

So she did.

One

Three Months Later

"Where the hell is Noah?" Jonah Flynn growled into his telephone and gripped his coffee mug fiercely in his free hand.

"He's…n-not in, sir."

His brother's administrative assistant, Melody, was audibly startled by his tone and he immediately chose to correct it. Jonah didn't raise his voice to his employees, ever. Honestly, the only person he ever shouted at was Noah. And he would direct his anger at his brother if he could find the bastard.

"I'm sorry for yelling, Melody. I didn't think he would be there. He's never in the office. What I really meant was do you know where he's gone to? He isn't answering his home phone and his cell phone goes directly to voice mail like he's got it turned off."

Melody hesitated on the line for a moment. Jonah could hear the clicking of her keyboard as she checked his calendar. "His calendar is wide-open, but he mentioned as he left that he was headed to Bangkok."

Jonah nearly choked on his latte. He swallowed hard and moved the cup out of his reach. "As in Thailand?"

"Yes, sir."

He took a deep breath to swallow his anger. He would not, could not, take this out on Melody. She'd already called him "sir" twice, which just felt wrong. Yes, he was the CEO, but he was also wearing jeans and a Monty Python T-shirt. Everyone just called him Jonah.

"Any idea when he'll be back?"

"No, but he did send me the number of the

hotel he's staying at. You could probably reach him there."

"That would be great, thanks, Melody." She read off the number and he quickly scratched it on his desk blotter before hanging up. He dialed it, getting transferred to his brother's suite without much trouble. Of course Noah didn't answer. He was probably frolicking with some exotic beauty. Jonah forced himself to leave a voice mail message that didn't betray the true reason for his call and hung up in disgust.

Thailand.

If he'd had any second thoughts about Noah being involved in his current mess, they immediately dissipated. If the preliminary accounting reports he was looking at were correct, his little brother had just taken off to Southeast Asia with three million dollars that didn't belong to him.

Jonah leaned back in his leather chair and gently rubbed his temples. This was not good.

The timing was never good for embezzlement, really, but his brother had just royally screwed him over in more ways than one. Noah didn't spend much time in the office; his role in the company was to please their mother and nothing else. But Noah knew—he *knew*—that they were close to wrapping up the deal with Game Town. The auditor they'd hired was showing up today. Today!

This could ruin everything. It wasn't a huge amount in terms of the numbers that ran through the company, but his brother wasn't smart and took it in one big chunk, transferring it to some offshore account he had in the Caribbean. Anyone with an interest would run across it eventually. Game Town was hiring FlynnSoft to manage their monthly game subscription service. Who would want the company handling their money to have issues like that? Jonah certainly wouldn't do it if the roles were reversed.

This needed cleaning up and fast. As much as he didn't want to, he could rearrange his assets for some cash and cover the loss. He would take it out of his brother's hide later. Maybe make him sell his overpriced European sports car. Perhaps even make him do some actual work at FlynnSoft for free until he paid off the debt.

But Noah *would* pay for this. By the time Jonah

was done with him, his little brother would wish he'd simply called the cops.

But he wouldn't. Not on his brother. And not for any love he had for his useless sibling, but for concern for their mother. Angelica Flynn had a degenerative heart condition and couldn't take much stress. If Noah, the baby and undoubtedly favorite child, ended up in jail, she'd have one hell of an attack. If she found out Noah was turned in by his own brother, he had no doubt she'd drop dead from the strain and embarrassment. In the end, it would all be Jonah's fault and he refused to be the bad guy in this.

He would handle his brother without their mother ever finding out.

Publicly, Jonah could deal with this however he wished. As a privately owned gaming company he had that luxury. Thank heavens he hadn't taken people's advice to go public. The move could make him a fortune overnight, but he'd also have shareholders and a board of directors to answer to. He could even be fired, losing control of the empire he'd started in his college dorm room.

No way. FlynnSoft was his and Jonah didn't answer to anyone, especially some pompous suits who thought they knew better than he did how to run his company. He'd bail FlynnSoft and his brother out one way or another. His employees deserved as much. And they deserved the money this new contract could bring in. *If* Noah hadn't just blown it.

What a mess.

Jonah flopped back into his executive chair and let his gaze drift over to the framed photograph that sat on the edge of his desk. In it, a Blue Morpho butterfly sat sunning itself on a clump of bright yellow flowers.

He'd gotten more than a few odd looks since he'd brought the picture into the office. Jonah wasn't exactly a nature buff. He'd spent his entire adolescence focused on video games and girls, both of which could be enjoyed in the climate-controlled comfort of his bedroom.

Of course, he couldn't tell anyone why it was really there. How do you explain a night like that to people? You just couldn't. They wouldn't believe you. If it wasn't for the proof inked into his skin, he might've believed she was a tequila induced hallucination. His gaze dropped to his right hand and the tattoo etched into the web of skin between his thumb and index finger. His fingertip grazed over the slightly raised design, tracing it as he'd done that night, only then it was across the silky skin of her chest. His half of the heart.

The other half had disappeared with the woman in the butterfly mask. He'd never anticipated a company Mardi Gras party at his loft would turn into an unforgettable night of body shots, anonymous sex and late-night tattoos. But for some reason, she, whoever she was, had gotten under his skin almost instantly. Everything from her soft gasp as he licked the salt from her throat to the way she'd begged for him to take her was etched into his mind.

Even with all the crap going on with Game Town, he couldn't help but let his thoughts drift to her again. She'd asked him for one night. No names, no personal details. Pure fantasy. Her multicolored glitter butterfly mask had obscured everything but her sleek, brunette ponytail, the full pout of her lips and the bewitching emerald green of her eyes.

How, exactly, had he decided that letting her walk out of his life was a good idea?

Jonah had been an idiot. He could see it now. For years, he'd gone through a lineup of women. They were all beautiful. Many were successful or talented in one way or another. They were drawn to his business success and the glamorous lifestyle he could provide. Most men would be content with the kind of woman who would throw herself at them, but he never was. He would inevitably get bored and move on. He'd actually earned a reputation as one of Manhattan's Most Eligible and *Elusive* Bachelors.

But his butterfly had kept his interest. Even three months later, he still found himself thinking about her. Wondering where she was. Who she was. Trying to figure out if the real woman could ever measure up to his memory of her. She'd insisted that the next morning he wouldn't want her anymore, like she would turn into a pumpkin at the stroke of midnight. Was it just the fantasy he craved? If he'd seen her face and known her name, would she have been relegated to the list of women he'd loved and forgotten? He didn't know.

Jonah ran his hand through the long strands of his dark brown hair and gripped the back of his skull. He needed to let this go. Let her go. If he kept looking down the blouse of every woman he met searching for that tattoo, eventually he'd get slapped. Or sued. Maybe arrested.

He simply couldn't help it.

With a sigh, Jonah turned back to his computer. He needed to focus. Noah would eventually come home and suffer mightily, but until then, he needed to clean up the mess. He searched through his contact list for his accountant, Paul. He'd be able to move his assets around and get the cash he needed. He always made sure his money worked as hard for him as he did for it and invested heavily, unlike his brother, who burned through money buying silly toys.

He could get the cash; it just might take a few days for the wheels of finance to turn.

In the meantime, he'd have to find a way to stall the forensic accountant Game Town was sending over. Someone would be showing up this afternoon at two. No one had mentioned the auditor's name, so he had no idea who, or what, to expect. His strategy would rely heavily on who showed up.

If the auditor was male, Jonah would drag his dusty golf clubs from the closet and take the guy out. He hated golf, but found it to be an important social tool in the business world. Few company honchos got together to play *Madden* on their Xbox. It was a pity. Instead, they would play eighteen holes; he'd buy the auditor some drinks. Steaks. Whatever. Perhaps if the guy was hung over enough, the numbers would take longer to crunch.

If the auditor was a woman, there would be a different tactic. The golf clubs would stay in the closet, but the charm would be on in full force. Regardless of whether she had three eyes and a hunchback or looked fresh from the Parisian runways, Jonah's charisma would carry him through. Since the age of fifteen, he'd had a way with women. A gift, he supposed, and one he made good use of. Dinner and drinks would still be involved, but the ambience would improve greatly.

He wouldn't have to lay a hand on her. The last thing he needed was the woman running back to Game Town with that tale. No, Jonah wouldn't go there. The right smile, some intense eye contact and a few compliments would go far, especially with a mousy accountant who wasn't used to the attention. If he planned this right, he'd have her so hot and bothered she wouldn't be able to remember her own name, much less see the problems with the financial reports.

No matter what, Jonah would come out on top. If he had to sit down with Carl Bailey, the CEO of Game Town, and explain what was going on, he would, but if it could be avoided, he'd gladly play eighteen holes or take a lonely accountant to the theater.

He made a note to ask his assistant, Pam, what shows were playing on Broadway at the moment. He wasn't a big fan of musicals, but he found most to be tolerable enough. Except *Cats*. He wasn't making that mistake a second time. That was a phenomenal waste of four hundred dollars, which was saying a lot, given he'd easily spend that much in a week on supplies for the gourmet coffee bar they added on the twenty-third floor.

Speaking of which, he eyed his now-cold coffee with dismay. He'd get a refill and a bagel after he talked to Paul. Picking up the phone, he dialed his accountant and mentally cleared his calendar for the next week. He'd be busy courting the Game Town auditor.

Jonah just prayed it was a woman. He really hated golf.

Surely her boss was a closet sadist. There was no other explanation for why he'd send her to FlynnSoft for two to three weeks. Tim could've sent anyone. Mark. Dee. But no, he had to send Emma. She was the only one who could handle herself in that environment, he said.

Slipping her hand inside the doorway to her closet, she flipped on the light switch and stepped inside. Tim was full of it. He just wanted to see her squirm. She liked to think that she'd been hired for her top grades at Yale and her recommendations from professors, but she had a sneaking suspicion her father had gotten involved and made it happen.

Tim likely resented some rich kid getting dropped into his department against his will and enjoyed making her miserable as a result. It made her more determined than ever not to give him that satisfaction. She was going to do a good job. No—a *great* job. She would not get sucked into FlynnSoft's corporate hippie attitude. She would not fall prey to *Jonah Flynn, Golden God* and his seductive smile.

Not that the notorious CEO would waste any of his smoldering looks on Emma. She wasn't bad to look at, but the last gossip blog she'd seen had him coming out of a restaurant with a model she'd recognized from her lingerie catalog. She simply couldn't compete with abs of steel and breasts of silicone. And she wouldn't even try.

A man like Jonah Flynn was of no interest to her, anyway. He embodied everything her mother, Pauline, had warned her about. *Don't make the same mistakes as Cynthia did*, she'd say. Her older sister hadn't died because of poor choices—a plane crash had done that—but when those choices came to light after her death, the family had been scandalized. Emma had grown up as her sister's polar opposite as a result.

If Tim was being absolutely honest with her, she'd bet that's why she got the job. Dee, although competent, was a tall, thin and attractive woman easily distracted by men. If Flynn even looked at her sideways, she'd be a puddle at his feet. Forensic auditors could not puddle. Emma probably wouldn't earn a second glance.

She eyed the neatly hung rows of clothing in her closet. Although FlynnSoft was a pioneer of the übercasual work environment, there was no way she was walking into that building while wearing jeans and flip-flops. Even if she stuck out like a sore thumb amongst the laid-back software designers, she was wearing one of her suits with high heels. Her sole concession to the casual environment would be leaving off the hosiery. Summer was just around the corner in New York and she preferred staying cooler in the heat.

She pulled a charcoal-gray suit and a light blue top from the rack and smiled in approval.

There was just something about the crispness of a freshly starched blouse and a smartly tailored blazer that gave her a much-needed boost of confidence.

It was just the armor she needed to go into battle against Jonah Flynn.

Battle was the wrong word, really. He wasn't the enemy. He was a potential contractor for Game Town. FlynnSoft had managed to build an extremely robust and efficient system for handling subscriptions and other in-game purchases for their addictive online game *Infinity Warriors*. Recently, they'd branched out offering the management of other online game system subscriptions to companies that needed help handling a high number of users or providing additional monetizing options. It allowed small software start-ups to focus on designing the game and let FlynnSoft manage the back end.

Before they went to contract, it was customary for the companies to have a forensic accountant review the vendor's records to ensure everything was shipshape. Carl Bailey, the man who started Game Town twenty years earlier and now headed up the board of directors, hated surprises.

Although FlynnSoft had a sterling reputation, the old man had a general distrust of a company where a suit and tie were not standard issue. Bailey wasn't getting into bed with any company he didn't think was up to snuff, even if paying Flynn was cheaper than developing the capability in-house. She was to go over everything with a fine-tooth comb.

Emma would be welcomed and provided everything she needed to do the job, but at the same time, no one liked an auditor nosing around. She might as well wear a big red button that read I Can Ruin Your Life.

That was a pretty unfair generalization. She could only ruin their lives by calling to light their own misdeeds. If they were good boys and girls, she couldn't get them into trouble.

Her mother had pounded that much into her head as a teenager. *Never say or do anything you wouldn't want printed on the front page of the newspaper*, she was always saying.

Before her sister, Cynthia, died in a plane

crash, she'd been engaged to the owner of the *New York Observer*, Will Taylor. He was also the business partner of their father, George. That newspaper was delivered to her childhood home every morning, and to this day, Emma lived in fear that something she did might actually turn up there. The scandals of the remaining socialite daughter of the Dempsey family were news worth printing.

So far, so good.

With a quick glance at the clock, Emma left her closet and started getting ready. She had to be at FlynnSoft at two to meet with Mr. Flynn at his insistence.

Normally, she would've simply worn what she'd put on to go to work that morning, but she came home at lunch to change. It was nerves. Her outfit that morning was more than suitable, but she felt this need to put on something else before she went over there. To get every hair in place.

After thirty minutes of primping, Emma gave herself one last inspection. Her brown hair was twisted into a tight bun. After David moved out, she chopped it off at her shoulders in typical female defiance, but it was still long enough to pull up. Her makeup was flawless—fresh looking, not too heavy. She could still see the faint specks of freckles across her nose, which she hated, but could do nothing about.

The suit was loose because of her recent stress-induced weight loss, allowing it to hide any unfortunate bumps she didn't want to share. The blouse she wore under the coat was a flattering shade of blue and more importantly, the neckline was high enough to hide her tattoo.

The half of a heart that was inked into her chest above the swell of her left breast wasn't the only evidence of the night she'd made the mistake of letting herself go, but at the moment, it was the hardest to hide. That wouldn't be the case much longer.

Like a little devil sitting on her shoulder, Harper told her to have fun that night. And she certainly did. She hadn't intended to take it that far, but there was something about her masked hero that she couldn't resist. Before she knew it, they were having fantastic sex in the laundry room and walking down the streets of New York in the middle of the night in search of adventure.

Every time Emma washed her clothes and felt the cold metal of the washing machine against her skin, a flush of embarrassment would light her cheeks on fire. She had done her best to forget about it and the tequila had done a good job turning the experience into a fuzzy, dreamlike memory, but still, it crept into her mind from time to time. If it hadn't been for the bandage on her chest when she awoke the next morning, she might've convinced herself it had never happened.

But it had. She'd allowed herself to do anything and everything she wanted to do. She'd let David's words strike too deeply and questioned everything about her life, when in truth there was nothing wrong with the way she lived. She did everything a proper Upper East Side woman was supposed to do. She was educated, well-spoken, polished and elegant. She took pride in her work as a CPA. It was true that no one would ever describe her as the life of the party, but her escapades would never show up on the front page of the local paper, either.

In retrospect, it took one uninhibited night to prove that she was okay with being that kind of woman. There was no glory in being like her older sister, who followed each pleasurable impulse and left her family mired in scandal after her death. Then again, that one night was enough for the repercussions to echo through her entire life. She could keep it under wraps for now, but eventually everyone would find out.

And of course, the tattoo remained. Emma had considered getting it removed, but it had become her personal reminder of how dangerous the wrong choices could be. Every time she even thought about breaking out of her shell, she could look at her tattoo and remember what a bad idea it was. It was a slippery slope she was determined not to go down again. She would not become her sister and shame her family. It didn't matter how good or right it might feel in the moment.

But in keeping it, she had to work hard to ensure it stayed covered, especially in a professional setting. Or near her mother, who felt tattoos were only for bikers and inmates. Emma had tripled her ownership of high-collared tops the last few weeks. She worried about the challenge of her summer wardrobe as the temperature climbed, but she had to deal with the FlynnSoft job first.

Emma was just thankful she'd gotten hers in a place she could hide easily, unlike her hero with his tattooed hand. There was no way he could disguise his half of the heart, although she wondered how he would explain it. He was at a FlynnSoft party, so he was potentially an employee, like Harper was. She supposed that in the laid-back corporate environment, a tattoo was no big deal. Might even be a requirement.

It was just another reason to be nervous about her assignment.

At any moment, he could appear. An engineer, a programmer, hell, even the janitor. She didn't know a thing about him and had no real way to find him other than the tattoo. She'd shared a few choice details of the night with Harper, and her friend had been on high alert to discover the man's identity since then. She hadn't been as willing to let the romantic fantasy go, especially when Emma confided in her about her predicament.

A few weeks after the party, at the family Easter dinner, Emma took one look at the spiral ham and went running down the hallway to the powder room. After two more weeks of denial and antacids, she realized she had more than a tattoo to show for her wild night—she was having her anonymous hero's baby! And had no way to contact the father and tell him.

In the last three months, there were no tattooed hands to report at FlynnSoft, at least in the marketing or accounting departments, where Harper spent most her time. The odds were that even if the man worked at FlynnSoft last February, he was gone now if Harper hadn't found him. That meant Emma was on her own with this baby, whether she liked it or not. She would tell her family soon. Eventually. When she couldn't hide her belly any longer.

Another glance at the clock proved that she couldn't delay any longer, as much as she might want to. She brushed her fingers over her hair and grabbed her purse from the table by the front door. With a fleeting look down her blouse, she opted to button her shirt one notch higher.

Just in case.

Two

It was an easy trip down to the FlynnSoft building, as she'd been there several times meeting Harper for a lunch date. They occupied the top five floors of one of the high-rises a few blocks from her apartment. The lobby was like many others with sleek, modern furniture and large LCD screens playing video clips about the company and scenes from the various video games they produced. The only difference, really, was the receptionist, who was wearing khaki shorts and a tank top. Her brown hair was pulled up into a ponytail that highlighted the multiple piercings in her ears.

If this was the first face of the company, she had no doubt things would go downhill from here. After checking her in, the woman gave her a temporary access badge and walked her back to the elevators. She showed her how to wave her badge over the sensor, allowing her to select the twenty-fifth floor, where the executive offices were located.

Emma considered stopping on the twenty-fourth-floor business wing to see Harper, but she didn't have time. They'd see each other plenty over the next few weeks, she was certain. Instead, she pushed the button that read 25 and closed her eyes. As the elevator rose, Emma could feel her anxiety rising, as well. She wished she knew why. She was more than capable of doing this job and being successful. She was an excellent auditor and accountant. Harper had done nothing but praise the company and everyone she worked with. Everything would be fine.

Exiting onto the twenty-fifth and top floor of the building, Emma headed down the hallway to the right as she'd been directed. Pausing in one of the doorways with a placard that read

Gaming Lounge, she watched a couple of employees playing foosball. In any other company, the large space would be a conference room, but here, there was a pool table, a *Ms. Pac-Man* machine and some beanbag chairs arranged around a big-screen television.

The players stopped their game to look over at her, staring as though she were wearing a clown suit instead of well-tailored gray separates. Emma quickly started back down the hallway to avoid their gazes. As though they had room to judge with their Converse and baseball caps.

She finally came to a large desk at the end of the hallway. A woman in a spring sundress with reddish-blond hair sat at it, talking into a headset and typing at her computer. She gave a quick glance to Emma and ended her call.

"You must be the auditor sent by Game Town." She stood and grinned, offering her hand over the desk.

Emma accepted it with a self-conscious smile. "Yes, I'm Emma Dempsey. How did you guess?"

The woman laughed, her eyes running over

Emma's professional outfit a second time. "I'm Pam, Jonah's assistant. He stepped down the hall, but he should be back any second. Can I get you a drink while you wait? A latte or a soda or something?"

Emma arched a confused eyebrow and shook her head. She didn't want any of the staff going to any trouble on her behalf. Some companies went to great lengths to kiss up to auditors and she didn't want to start out setting that kind of precedent. "No, thank you."

"Okay, but if you change your mind just let me know. We have a coffee bar on the twenty-third floor in addition to a Starbucks on the ground level. I'm sure you'll get the full tour, but while you're here, we hope you'll make use of all our employee amenities. We also have a gym, several game rooms and a pretty decent cafeteria with a salad bar where employees can eat at no charge. All the vending machines are also free to keep our programmers awake and productive."

"Wow." There wasn't really a better word for it. Emma had read in magazines about how Jonah Flynn was some sort of modern business pioneer who was changing everything. That he strived to create a workplace where people wanted to go so that staff would be happier and more productive. A casual work environment was only one piece. Apparently, a foosball table and free caffeinated beverages were another.

"This is a great place to work. Hopefully you'll enjoy your time with us." Pam walked out from behind her station and Emma noticed she was barefoot with sparkly, hot pink nail polish. At this point, that detail was no longer a surprise. Padding softly across the plush carpet, she escorted Emma to a set of double doors a few feet away. She pushed one of the heavy oak panels open, and then stepped back and gestured for her to go inside. "Have a seat and Jonah will be with you shortly."

The door closed silently behind her, and Pam and her toes disappeared, leaving Emma alone in Jonah Flynn's office.

As instructed, she quickly settled into one of the black leather guest chairs, crossing her ankles and holding her portfolio across her lap. She couldn't help but look around as her fingers nervously drummed against the notebook.

The office was massive with impersonal executive-type furniture that was very similar to the decor of the lobby. Glass and chrome, black leather, bookshelves with awards and books he'd probably never read. There was a large conference table that ran along the length of the floor-to-ceiling windows overlooking an amazing view of Manhattan.

She wasn't quite sure what she was expecting to find in the notorious CEO's office—perhaps a stripper pole and a *Donkey Kong* machine—but it all seemed to fit the space in a generic way aside from the giant cardboard cutout of what must be one of his video game characters. Emma was unfamiliar with it, but it looked like some kind of blue troll in battle armor.

There were only a few unexpected details. A photograph of a butterfly on his desk. A world's greatest boss trophy on the shelf behind his chair. A child's crayon drawing addressed to "Mr. Jonah" pinned to his corkboard. She was pretty certain he didn't have children, but she only knew what the gossip bloggers reported, which could be far from the truth.

"Miss Dempsey. Sorry to keep you waiting," a man's voice called out to her from over her shoulder.

With a nervous smile, Emma got up from her chair and turned to face him. He was standing in the doorway, taking up most of the space with his broad shoulders. Shoulders that were covered in a clingy brown T-shirt with what looked like some cartoon knights on the front. He was wearing loose-fitted jeans with a torn-up knee and well-broken-in high-top Converse sneakers. And a Rolex. She could see the large diamonds on the face from across the room as he held his drink.

What a contradiction. Software. Foosball. Jeans. Diamonds. You didn't run into this kind of CEO every day.

As he came closer, she only had a moment to register the face she'd seen in so many magazines: the distinctive dark brown hair with the undercut shaved on the sides, the deep blue eyes that seemed to leap from the glossy pages, the crooked smile that was endearing and arousing all at once. All of it was coming at her, full speed ahead.

Letting her business training kick into gear, she held out her hand. "A pleasure to meet you, Mr. Flynn," she said.

Jonah reached out to her, gripping her with a warm, firm shake. His dark eyes seemed to be appraising her somehow, a faint smile curling the corners of his mouth. If she didn't know better, she'd say he looked pleased about something.

"Call me Jonah. And the pleasure is all mine," he said, his voice as deep and smooth as melted dark chocolate with the hint of a British accent curling his words.

"Emma," she reciprocated, although the word barely made it across her tongue. Emma suddenly felt very aware of herself. Of him. Of the newly uncomfortable temperature of the room that made tiny beads of perspiration gather at the nape of her neck. His cologne tickled her nose, a spicy male scent that was infinitely appealing and somewhat familiar.

She tried to swallow, but a thick lump had

formed in her throat. She couldn't even speak while he continued to touch her. Did he have this effect on every woman or was she just that desperate after three months of celibacy and her pregnancy hormones conspiring against her?

Jonah Flynn was everything she expected him to be and then some. The magazines truly hadn't done the man justice. He was handsome without being too pretty, with hard angles and powerful, lean muscles flexing beneath the cotton of his shirt as he reached out to her. His every move was smooth and deliberate, exuding power and confidence even in a T-shirt and jeans. You just couldn't capture that in a picture.

She was blushing; she knew she had to be. How embarrassing. This was not going well at all. She had set out to prove to Tim that she could handle this assignment and here she was, practically mute and drooling after only a few seconds in the CEO's presence. Her clothes should be too big, since she had instantly transformed back into an infatuated twelve-year-old girl.

She needed to pull it together—and now. Emma broke eye contact to collect herself. Casually gazing down, she caught a glimpse of red, then recognized the other half of her tattoo etched into Jonah Flynn's hand.

Emma immediately began to choke.

Perfect. He'd never get the contract with Game Town if he killed the auditor on the first day.

Jonah quickly escorted the woman to a chair and buzzed Pam to bring her a bottle of water. He wasn't quite sure what just happened. One minute, she was smiling and shaking his hand, the next she was hyperventilating and turning bright red. Maybe it was an allergic reaction. He'd have Pam take the flower arrangement on his conference table to her area just in case. Wasn't there an EpiPen in the kitchen first aid kit? That would be his next move.

She'd calmed down a bit once she sat. Maybe she'd just swallowed her gum. No. She had pearl earrings and crossed ankles despite her inability to breathe. She definitely wasn't the kind of woman who chewed bubble gum at work. If at all.

Pam breezed through the door with the water,

which Emma gratefully accepted. Jonah held out his hand for Pam to stand by until he was certain the woman would recover.

Emma took a few breaths, a few sips and closed her eyes. Things were improving. He waved Pam off, but knew she'd be poised and ready if she were needed.

He knelt down in front of Emma, watching with concern as her breathing stabilized and her color began returning to normal. At least, he supposed it was normal. The woman was awfully pale, but his expectations were skewed by spray-tanned celebutantes who usually sported an orange undertone to their skin. No, he decided. Pale was normal.

Once she was no longer deprived of oxygen, he had to admit she was quite pretty. She had silky brown hair that begged to be hanging loose around her shoulders, but she'd forced it into submission in a knot-like bun. She had an interesting face, almost heart shaped, with full lips and creamy skin she didn't hide under a ton of makeup.

From what he could see of her figure beneath

that dowdy suit, she had ample curves in all the right places. Although he'd been photographed with the occasional model type, he gravitated toward the lingerie and swimsuit girls because they were equipped with the assets he was looking for.

Completing his inventory, he noticed her nicely manicured nails and naked ring finger. A single woman would be much easier to work his charms on.

This might not be the worst couple of weeks after all. Keeping Emma's mind off the books could turn out to be a pleasurable experience for them both.

"Are you okay?" he asked once she'd drained half the water bottle and he was certain she could speak again.

Emma swallowed hard and nodded, although her eyes were glued to his hand as it rested on her knee. "Yes, I'm sorry about that."

Following her gaze, he immediately removed his hand and stood up, allowing her some personal space. "Don't apologize. Is there anything Pam or I can do? Move the flowers, perhaps?"

"Oh no," she insisted. "I'm fine, really. Please don't worry about me."

She was the kind of woman who didn't like to be fussed over. Jonah made a mental note. "Okay, well, back to business, then." He rounded his desk and sank into the soft leather of his chair. "The Game Town people said it should take you a few weeks to go through everything."

"Yes." She nodded. "Perhaps less if the records are easily accessible and someone on staff can assist me with questions."

"Of course. I'll alert the finance people to have everything ready for you tomorrow. I'm sure they'll be happy to assist you with anything you need. You have our full cooperation. Everyone is very excited about this potential partnership with Game Town."

"I'm glad to hear it. I'm ready to get started."

Jonah arched an eyebrow, but quickly dropped it back in line. What was the rush? He *would* get an auditor who was hell-bent on getting the job done when it was the last thing he wanted. "How about we go on a tour first?"

"That's not necessary," she said, her answer

almost too quick. "I'm sure you have more important things on your agenda. If Pam can point me to my desk, I'm sure I can make do."

If Jonah didn't know better, it sounded like she was trying to dismiss him. Women never dismissed him. He wasn't going to let this one buck the trend. "Nonsense," he insisted, pushing out of his chair to end the argument. "I've got some time and I want to make sure you're settled."

Emma stood, somewhat reluctantly, and walked out of the office ahead of him. Despite her stiff manners, she moved fluidly and gracefully as a woman should. The curves of her rear swayed tantalizingly from left to right as she walked in her high heels to the door. Maybe that suit wasn't so bad after all. It fit nicely, hugging her hips just tight enough. He'd prefer to see her in a pair of clingy jeans and a tight little T-shirt, but the suit was growing on him. As were other things.

He took a deep breath to stifle the thoughts and pulled up alongside her once they started down the hall. "I'm sure you saw our gaming lounge on your way in. Each floor has one."

They paused at the doorway and he couldn't help but beam with pride. It was one of his favorite innovations. He probably spent as much time in these rooms as anyone. It was good for the spirit to break away for a while. It was refreshing and gave new enthusiasm to tackle the workload.

"That's very nice." Emma's voice was cold and polite.

She seemed decidedly disinterested and it annoyed him. She should be impressed like everyone else. *Forbes* magazine had done an article on his game lounges and sky-high productivity levels. It was groundbreaking territory. Certainly it should evoke more interest than her watery, patronizing smile suggested. Perhaps if he made it more personal? "What's your favorite video game? We have quite a collection here outside of the ones we produce in-house."

"I'm sorry. I don't play video games."

Jonah tried not to frown. Surely in this day and age everyone had a favorite game. Even his grandmother played bridge on the computer. "Not even *Super Mario Brothers* when you were a kid? *Sonic the Hedgehog*? *Tetris*, even?"

She shook her head, sending a dark strand of hair down along the curve of her cheek. It gave her a softness he found quite a bit more attractive than the uptight accountant thing she had going with that bun. Wearing her hair down around her shoulders would be infinitely more appealing. Seeing the brown waves tousled across one of his pillowcases would be even better. Although that couldn't be a part of his plan while the Game Town deal was pending and she worked under his roof, it didn't mean he couldn't continue to pursue her later.

Emma immediately tucked the rogue strand behind her ear and opened her mouth to ruin the fantasy he'd built in his head. "I was raised not to waste time in idle pursuits."

This time he had to frown. Idle pursuits. *Hmph.* His video game obsession as a child had blossomed into a multimillion-dollar video game empire. Not exactly idle. He wondered what she did with her time that was so superior. She certainly couldn't spend all her weekends feeding the hungry and knitting blankets for the homeless. Sweet ass or no, she was starting to work his nerves. "All work and no play can make for a dull girl."

Emma turned to him with a blankly polite expression. "There's no sin in being dull. Is it better to have scandal chasing your tail?"

"No, but it's certainly more fun." He couldn't help the sarcastic retort. The tone of condescension coming from her full, soft peach lips was a contradiction that set his teeth on edge. It was public knowledge that Jonah had scandal chasing his tail on more than one occasion. If nothing else, it kept a man on his toes.

Emma turned away from the game room and continued down the hall.

This time, watching her walk away was not nearly as enticing, as he'd been dismissed again. Containing his aggravation, he moved quickly to pull alongside her. Taking a breath, he decided to start over. She might be grating his nerves, but Emma was his pet project for the next few weeks.

"You'll be sitting on the twenty-fourth floor with the finance group while you're here. Before we go down there, let's stop by the twenty-third floor and I'll show you the coffee bar. I know I always need something to perk me up midafternoon."

"Mr. Flynn—"

"Jonah," he pressed with the smile that always got him his way where women were concerned.

"*Jonah*, this really isn't necessary. I'm sure someone other than the CEO can show me the coffee bar and the gym and the cafeteria. Right now, I really just want to get out of your hair and start to work."

He mentally amended his prior statement—his smile usually got him his way. Emma seemed immune. He sighed in resignation and held out a hand to escort her to the elevators. How was he supposed to charm this woman when she wouldn't let him? It was downright frustrating. "I'll just show you the area where you'll work, then."

They were silent as they waited for the elevators, which were running slowly just to spite him today. He had to admit he preferred her quiet. When her mouth was closed, she was attractive and graceful with just a touch of mystery in the green eyes that appraised him. When she spoke, it became abundantly clear that they came from two very different schools of thought where business and pleasure were concerned.

Jonah didn't know if it was better or worse that he found her perfume so appealing. Actually, as he anxiously watched the digital numbers of the elevator climb, he began to wonder if it was a perfume at all. The scent was more like a clean, fresh mix of shampoo and a lady's hand cream. It suited her more than the heavy stink of the perfumes that made his nose twinge. Much more delicate. Like the line of her collarbone that was barely visible at the V of her blouse.

The reflex to glance down her top for a tattoo was stifled by the blue dress shirt she wore. One less woman to slap him with a harassment suit, he supposed. Besides, Miss Goody Two-shoes was the least likely candidate to be his butterfly that he'd run across yet.

The doors finally opened and they took the short trip to the twenty-fourth-floor finance department. As they walked, he noticed Emma's gaze didn't wander like so many other visitors.

Normally people were interested in the untraditional workings of FlynnSoft. Emma's vision was fixed like a laser in front of her. Her intensity was both intriguing and a touch disconcerting. Would she be this focused on the financial reports?

He stopped at a visitor's office and opened the door. The small L-shaped desk took up much of the space with the computer setup and phone occupying one whole side. There was a corporate lithograph framed on one wall and a ficus shoved in the corner. It wasn't intended for long-term occupancy, but certainly it would be adequate for the short time she required it.

"This will be your home for the next few weeks. The desk is full of supplies, the phone is activated and there's a docking station for your laptop. If you need anything, the finance assistant, Angela, can help you. She's down the hall and to the left."

Emma watched him gesture, then nodded curtly. Another annoyingly dismissive gesture. The woman just couldn't wait for him to go away. What exactly was her problem? She was tight as a drum, every muscle taut, and anxious as though she itched to brush past him into the office and shut the door in his face. Why would such an attractive woman be wound up so damn tightly? She needed a drink. Or a good lay. Both couldn't hurt. He'd be happy to oblige if she'd give him the opportunity.

"Are you all right, Emma?"

Her head snapped toward him, a slight frown puckering the area between her eyebrows. Her green eyes searched his face for a moment before she spoke. "I'm fine."

The hell she was. But pushing her probably wasn't the best tactic this early on, so he let it slide. He didn't have to claim victory on the first day. He'd do it soon enough.

"You just seem a little uncomfortable. I assure you none of us bite." He planted his right hand on the door frame and leaned closer to her to emphasize his words. "You might even find you enjoy your time with us."

Emma's face went pale, her eyes focused on his hand and completely ignoring his persuasive charms. When she turned back to him, she flashed a saccharine smile. Sweetly artificial. "Of course. I'm just anxious to get settled in."

His hand fell heavy at his side. This wasn't going as well as he'd planned. He wasn't sure if she was deliberately being difficult or she was just like this normally. Paul had better be rushing that transaction because his wine-and-dine plan might not pan out the way he hoped. He'd just been assigned the only woman in Manhattan who was immune to him. Possibly even annoyed by him.

Maybe it was just the work environment. It was possible she stuck to strict business protocol and the casual interactions he was used to made her uncomfortable. All the better to get her away from the office, then. Give her the chance to let her hair down, kick off those heels and relax. He'd drop the dinner invitation, then leave her alone for the rest of the afternoon to stew over the possibilities. The anticipation alone would do a great deal of the work for him.

He glanced at his watch to lay it on thick. "I'd love to talk to you some more about your assignment, but I'm afraid I have a meeting in a few minutes. Would you be interested in having dinner with me tomorrow night?"

"No."

Jonah opened his mouth to suggest a restaurant and stopped cold. Had she just said no? That couldn't be right. "What?"

Her pale skin flushed pink and her eyes grew wide for a moment as she seemed to realize her mistake. "I mean no, *thank you*," she corrected, turning on her heel and disappearing into her new office with a swift click of the door.

Three

The following morning, Emma met Harper at the twenty-third-floor coffee bar before work. She'd barely slept the night before and was seriously in need of some caffeine.

"You look like hell," Harper said, always the honest one. When they'd first met at the sorority house, Emma wasn't quite sure what to think of her. Now she'd come to appreciate her candor. Most of the time.

"Thanks. Good morning to you, too."

They got into line and waited to place their orders. "What's wrong?" Harper asked.

"I just didn't sleep well last night."

Harper nodded and took a step forward to call out her customized coffee to the guy at the counter. Emma watched her, her brain trying to decide what she wanted to drink, but it simply refused to function like it should. She hadn't slept. Of course, she hadn't told Harper why.

She'd been in a nervous tizzy. Jonah Flynn. The playboy millionaire of the software world had the matching half to her tattoo. Fate had played a cruel joke. There was not a worse match on the planet for her, much less to father her child. It was just as well she'd kept her identity a secret. He most certainly would've been disappointed to see who she was beyond the tequila and the mask. And fatherhood for the most elusive bachelor in the five boroughs? Yeah, right.

And yet, as she lay in bed that night attempting to sleep, all she could think about was him. How he'd saved her from the creep. How a thrill of excitement had raced through her when he kissed her for the first time. She remembered his hands running over her body as though he couldn't get enough of her. After everything with David, it had felt incredible to be desired like that. It was a feeling that could easily become addictive and that meant it was dangerous.

She'd tried to forget about that night and had been mostly successful, but her body remembered. Being in the same room, touching him and breathing in his familiar scent had brought it all back. With a vengeance. In the dark of her bedroom, she could easily recall the sensations he'd coaxed from her body. Not once, in two years with David, had she ever responded like that. It was something raw, primal.

"Ma'am?"

Emma turned to the man at the counter, who was patiently waiting on her drink order. "Hot tea," she blurted. Although she probably needed the jolt of a black cup of coffee, she knew she wasn't supposed to have too much caffeine. That was a cruel irony for pregnant women everywhere.

The area was as miserably crowded as any Starbucks, so when their drinks were ready, they took them and their pastries, and went on their way back to their offices.

Harper seemed quite pleased with her new work arrangement. "I can get used to having you working here. I'd finally have someone to talk to. Everyone here is pleasant and all, but most of them have their heads in the clouds or their noses in a computer."

Emma had noticed that. Software designers were definitely different than most of the people she'd worked with. They were intensely focused, usually not even making eye contact or saying hello in the hallway. They were all on some mission, be it to fix a software bug or beat their nemesis at some video game. That or perhaps they just didn't know how to speak to women.

"Then why do you stay?" Emma asked. "We both know you don't need to work."

Harper narrowed her gaze at Emma, then shrugged. "I get bored doing nothing."

"You could always help Oliver. He might like having his sister there at the family business."

"Oliver doesn't need my help with anything. Besides, this place is fun. You'll get spoiled quickly. I save so much money with the free food. I was able to drop my gym membership, too, which saved me a bundle. Now I can use that money for Louis Vuitton handbags and trips to Paris, instead. I enjoy having income I earned on my own, not because of my last name. You couldn't get me to leave here and I hope you'll feel the same. We do need to make some adjustments to your wardrobe, though."

Emma looked at Harper's khaki capris and silky, sleeveless top, then down at her conservative suit and frowned. It was her favorite. She'd always thought the dark green had complemented her coloring. "I can't help it if everyone here dresses like college students. I refuse to assimilate. And don't you get your heart set on me being here past a few weeks. The minute I can get out of here, I will."

They paused at the elevator and Harper pushed the button. "Why are you so anxious to go? Is it that bad?"

It wasn't, but staying here a moment longer than she had to was courting disaster. Emma wondered how much she should tell Harper about yesterday. Harper was one of her best friends, but she was lacking in social couth.

Anything she told her would instantly be passed along to their friends Violet and Lucy, as well. From there, who knows who would find out. Emma wanted Jonah to stay in the dark about her identity for the time being and the best way to make that happen was to keep her friends out of the loop.

"I'm just not comfortable here."

"You're afraid of running into *him*." The remark hit a little too close to home for her taste. Harper always had a way of seeing too much where Emma was concerned. It made her an excellent friend, but left Emma little privacy, even in her own head.

There was no sense in denying it. "Yes, I'll admit it. It would be awkward, at best, to run into him. And at worst, a conflict of interest if anyone at Game Town found out. My entire report could be compromised if anyone thought I was personally involved with someone here."

"Or it could be the most wonderful thing ever. I thought you wanted to find him. You know, for the sake of the *B-A-B-Y*." She mouthed the last part silently.

Emma didn't respond. Harper was too wrapped up in her romantic ideas to see the situation objectively and there was no sense in explaining herself any further. She just stepped onto the elevator when the doors opened and sipped her hot tea.

"You've already seen him!" Harper accused.

She snapped her head to the side to confirm they were alone in the elevator. "What? No, of course not."

Harper was unconvinced by her response. "Who is it? Is he cute? What department does he work in?"

The doors opened to the twenty-fourth floor and Emma waved at her friend to be discreet as they stepped out. "Would you keep it down? I don't want everyone to know."

"Okay, but you've gotta tell me. I can keep it a secret."

Emma eyed her with dismay. She loved her friend, but honestly… "No, you can't."

Harper frowned and planted a hand defiantly on her hip. "Oh, come on. Why not? I mean, it isn't like it's the CEO or something. Bagging

Jonah would be quite gossipworthy, but anyone else is just run-of-the-mill office news. I don't know what the big dea—"

Emma could feel the color drain from her face and there was nothing she could do to stop it. Harper halted in her tracks, forcing Emma to turn and look back at her. Her friend's jaw had dropped open, her perpetual stream of words uncharacteristically on hold.

"Oh my God," she finally managed.

"Shh! Harper, really. It doesn't matter."

"The hell it doesn't!" Her voice dropped to a hushed whisper that was still too loud for Emma's taste. "Jonah Flynn? Seriously?"

Emma nodded. "But he doesn't know who I am or know anything about the baby. And I intend to keep it that way for now. You understand?"

Harper nodded, her mind visibly blown by her friend's news. "Jonah Flynn is the hottest man I've ever seen in real life. He and my brother are friends, and it took everything I had not to throw myself at him every time he came to the house.

I can't believe you two… How did you not jump into his lap when you realized who he was?"

"Have we met?"

Harper frowned. "You're right. A damn shame, though. What a prize to land. He was totally smitten with you."

"He's a player. I seriously doubt that."

"If you believe the gossip, then yes, Jonah Flynn is a notorious womanizer. But that's not the guy I've known over the years. And the guy you were with was willing to tattoo himself after one night together on the off chance it might reunite you someday. A playboy wouldn't have an inch of skin unmarked if that was what he did with everyone. You were special to him. Special enough for a guy that goes through women like tissues to take serious notice."

That was true. Emma hadn't spied another tattoo on what she'd seen of his body, then or now. But she refused to believe there was any kind of future with him. Even if he was interested in starting something, he wanted the woman she was that night. Not regular old Emma. And she swore she'd never be that woman again. So what was the point? Telling him who she was would just torture them both and ruin the memory of that night.

And yet she had to. Or did she? Her hand dropped protectively to her belly. If Jonah rejected Emma and their child, it could scar the baby forever knowing its father didn't want him or her. Would it be better to keep quiet? The idea was unsettling to her, but until she decided, not a word could get out. "You have to keep this a secret, Harper. No one can know. Not Violet, not Lucy, not your brother and especially not Jonah."

"Cross my heart." Harper sighed in disgust and Emma could see it was almost physically painful for her to say the words. "You'd better keep that tat of yours under wraps, though."

Emma straightened her collar nervously and started back down the hallway. "I don't make a habit of displaying my décolletage and have every intention of keeping it hidden. I'm here to do my job and get out."

"But what about the baby?" Harper trailed behind her.

"I don't know, Harper. What happened between us is over. Never to be repeated. Ancient history. I don't know that the baby will change that." Emma reached out and opened the door to her office. Sitting on her desk was a large crystal vase filled to overflowing with white lilies in full bloom. The warm scent of them was nearly overwhelming in the small space, making her happy that she was past her morning sickness. She'd never received a more beautiful bouquet of flowers in her life.

She stepped inside and plucked the card from the plastic prong. As she flipped open the envelope, she couldn't decide if she wanted them to be from Jonah or not. His attentions, although flattering, were pointless and even dangerous if he knew who she really was. Yet her impractical, inner girl couldn't help but wish they were from the handsome businessman.

"'To Emma,'" she read, her stomach aflutter with nerves and excitement. "'Welcome to FlynnSoft. I look forward to getting to know you better.' It's signed *Jonah*."

"Ancient history, eh?" Harper said, leaning in to sniff one of the flowers. "Are you so sure about that?"

* * *

Jonah came down the hallway from the elevator, coffee in one hand, bagel in the other, and paused outside his office. There was a large and quite stunning crystal vase of white Casablanca lilies sitting on Pam's desk. He frowned. He'd specifically ordered that type of lily for Emma because he felt they were a reflection of her: elegant, pure and refined. They didn't make any flowers that were stuffy and aggravating.

Plus, he thought she'd see right through roses. Lilies were different, exotic. He'd spent enough on them to catch the attention of even the most difficult to please female.

He would be the first to admit he typically didn't have to work that hard to woo the ladies. He'd been told that with his good looks and irresistible charm, the panties of every woman within a fifty-yard radius simply flew off. It made for an amusing visual, one he'd like to witness really, but he wasn't naive. He figured their interest in him probably had more to do with the fact that he was filthy rich rather than charming. Panties were consistently repelled by obscene displays of money.

But Emma was different. Her iron underwear stayed firmly in place when he was around. And given her stiff, overly polite demeanor and cutting tongue, they were probably chafing.

That was just not acceptable. The one time he needed his way with women to work without fail... The auditor Game Town hired was priority one even if charming her would take everything he had. He was willing to shift his tactics and restrategize his game plan, but in the end, he would be successful.

Even if right now, things didn't appear to be going so well. Emma had rejected the flowers and in record time. The odds of Pam receiving the same flowers on the same day were slim to none.

"Did Miss Dempsey bring those up here?" he asked.

Pam was beaming with the large bouquet perched on her desk. She seemed to really take pleasure in having them there where everyone who passed by, including her, could see them.

Well, at least someone was enjoying them. The money hadn't gone entirely to waste.

"Yes," she said. "She told me she was allergic and I should enjoy them. Aren't they pretty?"

He made a mental note to buy his assistant flowers more often. Make that all the administrative assistants. The occasional flowers probably appealed to them more than the *Ms. Pac-Man* machines, and he probably catered too much to the programmers with his corporate innovations. They couldn't function without the admin staff and something like that would be great for their morale.

"Lovely indeed." He continued past her desk to his office with his breakfast in hand and let the door slam behind him. Allergic, his ass. She swore yesterday that her choking fit had nothing to do with the flowers and he believed her. This was about her being stubborn. Never in his life had he run across a woman so resistant to him. It didn't make any damn sense.

Jonah settled into his chair, set down his food and fired up his computer with a stiff punch of his finger. It almost made him wonder if he'd romanced her before. Or one of her friends. She had the attitude of a woman who'd been loved and left by him or someone like him in the past.

But that couldn't be the case. Despite the lengthy list, Jonah had a great memory for names and faces. He'd never laid eyes on Emma Dempsey before yesterday. If she was bitter about men like him, it wasn't his doing.

But it would be his job to change her outlook. The deal with Game Town was riding on it. Even if he could get his hands on Noah and wring three million dollars from his neck, the transaction would be in the records.

His phone rang, an unknown number lighting up the display. Pam had put the call through, so he figured he wasn't about to be assaulted by a telemarketer.

"Jonah Flynn," he said into the receiver.

"Hey, it's your favorite brother."

Speak of the devil. Jonah took a deep breath before he said anything, choosing each word carefully. "I've told you before that Elijah is my favorite brother, but Noah, you're just the man I was looking for."

His brother chuckled on the line. They both knew the operations of FlynnSoft had nothing to do with Noah. He occupied an office. Drew a paycheck. On a rare occasion when he was bored with his other mysterious pursuits, he helped with charity golf tournaments and presented large, cardboard checks.

"What's so important that it couldn't wait until I came back from this trip? This call is costing me a fortune."

"What?" Jonah asked. "About three million dollars?"

The silence on the end of the line told him everything he needed to know. Noah had taken the money but didn't think anyone would notice it so quickly. Maybe any other time they might not have noticed it before he replaced it. But his timing sucked and Emma would find it, Jonah had no question.

"Listen, I don't care whether you blew it on hookers and fruity drinks or built schools for poor children. It doesn't matter. But I want it back right now."

"Yeah, that's a little iffy at the moment. I don't

exactly have it right now. But hopefully I will by the time I come home."

"And when will that be?"

"Two weeks at the most."

"Okay, fine. But if it isn't back in my hands—*in full*—within fifteen minutes of you arriving in the US, I'm going to take every penny out of you with my fist."

"Jonah, I—"

"I don't want to hear your excuses. You come up with three million bucks or I will make you so miserable you'll wish you'd stayed in Thailand. Am I clear?"

This time, Noah didn't try to argue. "Crystal. Have you told Mother?"

Now it was Jonah's turn to laugh. "No. And I have no intention of doing it unless I have to. You and I both know her heart can't take the stress, although it doesn't stop you from pushing the boundaries."

"I would never deliberately hurt Mother," Noah argued.

Jonah shook his head in dismay. "It doesn't

matter whether it's deliberate or not, you still do it. You never think of anyone but yourself."

"And you don't think of anyone but your employees and your company," Noah countered. "You practically ignore the whole family. When was the last time you went to the estate to visit her? Or came to my apartment? Or Elijah's place? You accuse me of blowing money on Thai hookers and you spend every bit of time and money you've got on vapid supermodels."

Jonah's jaw grew tighter with every word out of his youngest brother's mouth. If he had the time, he'd fly to Thailand right that instant just so he could punch Noah in the face. His brother seemed to think that this company had appeared out of thin air. That Jonah hadn't had to pour his heart and soul, in addition to all his free time, into building it and making it a success. When he did get to play, he played hard. Yeah, he didn't spend much time with his family, but they all had their own lives, too. None of them had knocked on his door recently, either.

"The company is important to me, yes. It supports a lot of people, including you in case you've forgotten. I have pride in what I've built and I'm not about to lose it because you're a thoughtless little prick. You do know the auditor from the Game Town deal is here, right? That your little stunt may have cost the company a huge, lucrative contract?"

"Oh hell," Noah swore. "I completely forgot about that. I didn't think—"

"No, you didn't think, Noah. You never do."

There was an awkward silence on the line for a few moments while Jonah took another deep breath.

"Do you think they'll find it?" he asked.

"Probably. You did everything short of highlighting the withdrawal with a yellow marker. But I'm trying to clean it up. Paul's moving some money around. Temporarily," he emphasized, "to cover the gap until you pay it back."

"I will pay it back, Jonah."

"Yeah, yeah," he sighed. "Just don't make me regret trusting you."

"I promise you won't."

"I'll see you when you get back," Jonah said, hanging up the phone.

He wanted to believe his brother, but it was hard. He was never a bad kid, just one who was used to getting his way. As the youngest, his pouty lip would melt their mother's heart in an instant, especially after Dad died. When he got older, people seemed to go out of their way to give him whatever he asked them for.

If Jonah was smart, he'd put Noah to work full-time on corporate fund-raisers. His best job fit might be applying that skill to encourage rich people to part with their money. In this economy, FlynnSoft wasn't able to raise as many outside dollars for charity. Noah might make the difference.

That is, if his unorthodox loan didn't cost them a huge contract and put all their donation programs on hold.

Jonah leaned back in his chair and took a bite of his bagel. The day was so complicated already and it wasn't even 9:00 a.m. yet. Two weeks. He had to figure out how to replace or bury the stolen money until Noah came back. And then find some way to put it back in without raising more flags.

Until then, he had to find a way to get around Emma's defenses. The direct approach wasn't working and he didn't want to strong-arm her. He'd never had to beg or coerce a woman to go out with him in his life and he wasn't about to start now. It didn't exactly set the right mood. He wanted her ready and willing, not even more stiff and distant than she already was.

It really was a shame. Emma was a beautiful woman. A sensual woman, although she seemed determined to keep that fully under wraps. He could tell by the luscious sway of her hips and the way her full lips parted slightly when he leaned near to her. She had a reaction to him. Certainly. She just wasn't willing to do anything about it. Yet.

But he could plant the seed. Get under her skin. Whether or not she agreed to let him wine and dine her, he was going to do everything in his power to make sure she went home every night and thought about him. Whether it was with irritation or suppressed lust, he didn't care. Either would be enough to help her lose focus, and that was the most important part.

It would take Paul a couple more days to get the money. Until then, he had some unofficial FlynnSoft business to tend to.

Popping the last of his bagel in his mouth, Jonah got up from the desk and went in search of his curvy, uptight auditor.

Four

Emma had rarely been as happy to get home as she was tonight. It seemed like no matter where she went or what she was doing, she would run into Jonah. Not like he was following her; he was just always there. She'd look up from the copier and see him down the hall talking to someone. He'd look at her and smile, the charming grin chipping away at her defenses before he turned back to his discussion. He was in the cafeteria, the coffee bar, passing her in the hallway…*constantly*.

And when Jonah wasn't there, she found her-self thinking about him anyway with a confusing mix of irritation and, if she was honest with herself, desire.

She didn't want to admit it, but no red-blooded woman could resist Jonah's charms. Emma had tried her best, but he was infuriatingly persistent and wearing her down. Their past didn't help. Knowing what he could coax from her body, knowing what it felt like to cling to him, uninhibited and anonymous, made it that much worse. She couldn't concentrate. The lines of the financial records blurred together, the math not adding up in her head no matter how many times she ran the figures. Her focus was not on the audit and it absolutely had to be—charming, sexy CEO be damned.

It was a relief to get home, the one place where she knew she was safe from Jonah Flynn. There was something about the feminine fabrics, soft throw pillows and cheerful colors that instantly made her entire body and mind relax. She'd decorated her Upper East Side apartment to look like a cozy retreat out of *Country Living* magazine, casual and inviting.

And yet, when she slipped out of her work

clothes and into something more comfortable, she realized she wasn't even safe from Jonah here. As she stood in the bathroom, clutching a worn T-shirt to pull over her head, she caught a glimpse of herself in the mirror. There, just above the bare swell of her breast, was the blasted tattoo staring back at her.

She could still see him standing there, his mask obscuring everything but the same boyish grin, sharp jaw and dark blue eyes that seemed to rid her of all her good sense.

"Let's get a tattoo," he'd said.

Emma hadn't realized they'd stopped on the sidewalk outside a tattoo parlor until he said that. It wasn't the kind of place she typically took notice of. Or had any interest in going to.

"Two halves of one heart," he'd lobbied and pressed the palm of his hand against the bare skin of her chest exposed by the low neckline of her top. His fingertips had gently curved around the edge of her breast, sending an unanticipated wave of pleasure through her. He had the uncanny ability to render her brain butter with the simplest touch.

"Right here." He'd traced his skin at the juncture of his thumb and index finger, then across her skin, showing how their touch would make the heart whole. "If we're meant to be together after tonight, I'll find you. And this heart will be how we'll recognize one another."

Emma's heart had swelled in her chest. His suggestion had been romantic and spur-of-the-moment and completely stupid. Not once in her life had she ever considered getting a tattoo, but that night had included a lot of firsts for her. With his hand gently caressing her and those ocean-blue eyes penetrating her soul, she couldn't help but follow him into the shop.

Looking in the mirror now, she let her fingertip trace the heart the way his had done. Just imagining it was his hand instead of her own sent a shiver of longing through her body and her skin drew tight with gooseflesh. He'd been the last man to touch her, three long months ago. Her realization that she was pregnant with the stranger's child had been a big enough disruption, making her physical needs easy to ignore, but now, knowing how close he was, it was as though her libido had flipped a switch.

Flustered by her wanton response to the ghost of a man she couldn't have, she pulled the T-shirt over her head and marched back into the living room to make dinner.

It was Tuesday and if she kept daydreaming, the girls would arrive and she wouldn't be ready.

Every Tuesday, Lucy, Harper and Violet gathered at Emma's apartment for dinner and their favorite television series. They took turns cooking or buying takeout. Tonight, she'd promised Lucy she would make her favorite baked ziti and she hadn't even boiled water yet.

In the kitchen, she busied herself by preheating the oven and gathering the ingredients for the family recipe. The ziti recipe was one of the few valuable things her older sister had taught her before she'd died.

Everything else she'd learned from her sister was more of a cautionary tale. She'd been sixteen when Cynthia died, barely dating herself, and yet the truth of her sister's secret life had scared her parents enough to clamp down on

Emma with an iron fist. She was hardly a problem child, but of course, Cynthia had always
seemed perfect on the surface, too.

When she was old enough to be in charge of
her own life, she'd thought about rebelling. Her
hunt for a sorority had been a start, but instead,
she went the other direction and chose Pi Beta
Phi, the sorority of proper, well-off ladies out
to do community service and build sisterhood.
She'd seen how her sister's scandal had hurt her
parents and she didn't want to be the one responsible for putting that look on their faces ever
again. When she finally lost her virginity in college, it was to a well-groomed, polite premed
major she'd been dating for nearly six months
and had hoped to marry. She pretended to be the
proper, sophisticated society darling her parents
wanted, and after a while, it just became who
she was.

She'd only really, truly let herself go that
once. Emma let herself do shots of tequila with
a stranger, licking salt from the musky skin of
his throat and sucking a lime from his full, soft
lips. From there, it was a slippery slope that led

to the tattoo on her chest and a positive pregnancy test on the back of the toilet. One night had ruined a decade of good behavior. She had no idea how she was going to tell her parents.

Emma opened the box of pasta and dumped it into a pot of boiling water with an unsatisfying splash. It had been so easy to let herself get carried away that night. Too easy. There was a part of her that understood how her sister could get so wrapped up in a passionate and illicit relationship while she was engaged to someone else. The pleasure and the excitement were enthralling. The other part of her knew there was nothing worth derailing her whole life for.

There was nothing she could do about the choices she'd made in the past, but she certainly wasn't going to make the same mistakes twice. Jonah Flynn was just the kind of man who could make her priorities get all out of whack. That made him dangerous. She would tell him about the baby once the audit was complete and she had done her job. He couldn't know the truth about her identity or the baby before then, which made it imperative that she not let her guard down around him.

"We're here!" Violet called out from the living room.

"I'm in the kitchen," she replied, giving the pasta a stir and setting the timer. Since she'd added the girls to the approved guest list with the doorman, they tended to show up with little warning. "It's nowhere near ready, sorry."

The girls came around the corner with paper sacks and set them on the counter. "We're not in a hurry," Harper insisted. "Anyway, I brought a bottle of chardonnay and Violet picked up some cheese and crackers to keep us busy until dinner is ready. The wine is just for us, of course."

Her best friends unpacked the items from the bags and set them on the counter. "Oh, and tiramisu," Harper admitted, pulling the seductive dessert from the bag. "I had to."

Emma groaned inwardly. "You said FlynnSoft has a gym, right? After all this I'm going to have to find it or I'll gain fifty pounds with this kid. Now that I've gotten my appetite back, I'm hungry almost all the time."

Harper smiled and nodded. "It's on the ground floor near the rear entrance. You can't miss it. There's usually no one in there after six or so. You can have it all to yourself."

"I don't know what you're complaining about," Lucy said. She reached out and put her hand on Emma's slightly rounded belly. "You look like you had a big lunch, not that you're over three months pregnant. I think you can afford some indulgent carbs."

"I'm glad you think so," Emma quipped. "Now open those crackers. I'm starving."

Violet opened the box of crackers while Lucy pulled wineglasses from the cabinet and the corkscrew from the drawer.

"So how is the FlynnSoft assignment going?" Lucy asked after Harper opened the bottle and poured her glass.

There was something about Lucy's tone that worried Emma. She turned away from the marinara sauce she'd made and frozen to look at Harper and knew instantly that she'd spilled the secret about Jonah to the others. Emma swore under her breath and returned to mixing the cheeses and seasonings into the bowl.

"I'll just presume you all are caught up on who Jonah is—thank you, Harper—and jump right into it. I have never met a man so persistent in my life. You should've seen his face when I told him I wouldn't go to dinner with him. It was as though I was the first woman in his life to ever tell him no."

"You probably were. I sure wouldn't tell him no," Violet spoke up.

"Well, someone needs to," Emma responded. "He's not a god. He can't get his way all the time. That kind of arrogance makes me crazy."

"I've never really thought of him as arrogant in the years I've known him," Harper said, shrugging. "He's confident, sure, very smart, of course. He knows what he wants and he goes after it. I find that attractive. But you're determined not to like him, so he could save puppies from burning buildings and you would find a reason to hate him for it."

Emma opened her mouth to argue, but knew there wasn't much point. It was true. Mostly.

She didn't hate him. She couldn't feel that way about the father of her child. But she had to find things wrong with him for her own protection. And if he was perfect, she'd make up lies in her head about all of Jonah's evil doings and pretend they were true. "It's better this way, trust me."

"Why, Em?" Lucy settled into a chair at the kitchen table. "And don't give me some story about your sister. We've all heard it before and know better than anyone that you're not your sister. You certainly aren't going to disappoint your parents with anything you do. You're a better person."

"There's no sense in punishing yourself for sins you've never committed," Lucy said.

Instead of answering right away, Emma drained the pasta and started mixing it with the sauce and cheese to put in the oven. What could she say to that? Was that really what she was doing? "I'm not punishing myself."

"Yes, you are," Harper insisted. "If not for your sister's sins, then for whatever you did at that Mardi Gras party. I think the punishment far outweighs the crime."

"That night was a mistake and I'll never be able to put it behind me. Don't you think getting impregnated out of wedlock by a stranger at a party will disappoint my parents?"

"They might not be thrilled, but grandbabies become a joy no matter what," Violet said.

"I'll remind you of that when you accidentally get pregnant by a man whose name you don't know, Violet."

"Listen, honey," Harper interjected. "I've made plenty of mistakes where men are concerned. But not even one of my best moments were as sexy or romantic as what you told me about your night with him. You jumped in with both feet and scared yourself. Okay, I get it. But that doesn't mean you have to stay out of the pool entirely. If you're not ready for the deep end, at least put your feet in. Test the waters. Letting your hair down every once in a while won't hurt anything. It might be good for you."

Popping the casserole dish in the oven, Emma dusted her hands off on her yoga pants and eyed her friends' wine with a touch of jealousy. If she didn't put an end to this discussion, her friends would continue to badger her and they'd miss the show they'd come over to watch. "That is all well and good, but I'm not getting in a pool of any kind with Jonah Flynn. Not that he'd want to once I'm huge and pregnant anyway."

"With *his* baby!" Lucy pointed out.

"It doesn't matter. Does he look like the paternal type to you? I've told you my reasons for avoiding Jonah, but if nothing else I've said convinces you, know that it's a major conflict of interest. I'm auditing FlynnSoft. If even so much as a whisper of a relationship pops up about Jonah and me, past or present, my credibility is shot. I'd probably lose my job and permanently damage the reputation I've worked so hard to build. No man, not even Jonah Flynn, is worth that. Not to me."

"Well, they're going to find out when the baby is born and everyone figures out what happened between the two of you. There's no avoiding that. Your only option is to tell Tim you can't do it. That would be the most forthright answer," Violet said.

"Technically. But *can't* isn't in my vocabulary.

I refuse to back down from this challenge, even if there's a risk."

Harper nodded in resignation and Lucy sighed. Emma hoped her friends would leave it alone, at least for the next two hours.

"Of course," Harper said with a smirk, "if I was going to sully my reputation and ruin my career for a man, it'd be for him."

Jonah was sitting at his desk Wednesday afternoon when his phone rang. He recognized the number as his financial advisor, Paul. Hopefully it was good news.

"Paul," he said. "Tell me what I want to hear."

There was a hesitation on the line that instantly told Jonah he was out of luck. "I'm sorry to tell you, Jonah, but it's going to take me at least two more days to get everything handled. We could look into getting a short-term loan to get you the money, but the banks are really tight on those lately with the market the way it is. I doubt it would come through any faster. Any chance you could borrow it from…um…"

"From my mother?" Jonah asked.

"She does have more liquid assets than you do. That's the only reason I would even suggest it."

Jonah sighed and shook his head. He wanted to keep this situation as close to his vest as he could. "I don't want Mother to know what Noah's done. Ask someone for three million dollars and they'll sure as hell want to know what it's for. At least she'd ask *me*. She'd give it to Noah without blinking."

"Then why didn't he just borrow it from her in the first place?"

Jonah ran his fingers through his messy hair. "I have no idea. The less I know about what he's up to the better. Listen, just move things as quickly as you can and I'll do what I have to on this end."

They wrapped up their conversation and Jonah hung up. He'd given Emma some space this morning, hoping maybe the money would come through and he wouldn't need to continue pursuing a woman who was clearly disinterested in him. It was fun for him, a challenge he'd never had to face before, but he couldn't spend all his time trying to woo the ice princess. He still had a company to run.

Apparently that task was back at the top of his to-do list for the day. He had some time on his calendar, so he slipped out from behind his desk and went in search of his elusive prey.

He spotted her on the twenty-fourth floor down the hall from her office. She was leaning over the copier, pressing buttons and eyeing the pages as they spat out. Jonah was tempted to come up behind her and whisper something in her ear, but nixed the idea. Somehow he thought that might earn him a slap or a knee to the groin.

Instead, he just watched her from a distance, admiring the curve of her calves highlighted by her knee-length skirt and four-inch heels. She held a pen gently to her full, soft lips, the lower one pouting just slightly and urging him to reach out and brush his mouth across hers.

The best thing about watching her from here was that her defenses were down. She was relaxed, a faraway daydreaming look in her eyes as the constant rhythm of the copier lulled her mind into thoughts about something other than accounting. He didn't know what she was thinking about, but the corner of her mouth curved in a smile. It made her face light up in a way he hadn't seen before. She was always so proper and guarded around him.

It was then that she turned to glance down the hallway and spotted him. Her green gaze ran over the length of his body for just a moment, her tongue darting quickly across her bottom lip. He thought he caught the slightest hint of something other than derision in her eyes, but before he could be certain, she snatched her papers from the copier, turned on her heels and started off in the other direction.

She was avoiding him again. No more avoiding.

Jonah marched up behind her. She was easy to catch with those high heels slowing her escape. He spied one of the janitorial closets just to her right and got a bad idea. Without so much as a hello, he wrapped one arm around her waist and opened the door, tugging her inside.

"What on *Earth*—" she shrieked in surprise, but quickly silenced when the door slammed shut and they were suddenly cloaked in the darkness of the small space.

The room was slightly musty, smelling of industrial cleaner and old cardboard, but the subtle scent of her lotion cut through it all and sent a spike of need down his spine. Memories of the night with his butterfly flooded his mind in an instant. He'd made love to her in the small, private space of his laundry room when no place else was available. If he'd had a second chance with her, he would've made up for it with a bed covered in satin sheets and rose petals. That's what she had deserved.

Again, like the laundry room, the janitorial supply room wasn't the best or most romantic choice, but he would take what he could get. He had no intention of trying to seduce her here, but if this was the only way he had of getting her alone to talk, so be it. He was tired of this game.

He tightened his arms around her waist and tugged her close to him so she couldn't get away. The closet was filled with any number of dangerous things she'd likely hurt herself with if she took a step back from him. She needed to stay right where she was. They were going to talk about what was going on whether she liked it or not.

So far, he was pleased enough with the situation. She was very still and quiet in his arms, albeit a touch stiff. He could hear the soft sound of her breathing, the rise and fall of her chest as she pressed futilely against him with her palms. He liked the feel of her in his arms more than he expected to. It felt natural and familiar somehow.

As his eyes adjusted to the dim light coming under the door, he was able to make out her silhouette and the soft contours of her face. What he could see of her was fighting this tooth and nail. Her eyes were squeezed shut, her lips tightly pressed together. Emma's shoulders were drawn up around her ears. She was strung tight as a drum, the comfortable woman from minutes ago completely forgotten.

"Relax, Emma. I'm not going to bite."

"I need to get back to work," she said, but there was half-heartedness in her voice that betrayed her. There was a part of her that was open to him. He didn't know why she was fighting it so hard. It could be quite an enjoyable experience for them both.

"I want to talk to you first. You've continued to avoid me and have left me with no choice but to abduct you and make you listen to what I have to say."

"I'm not talking to you in a closet with the lights off. It's inappropriate." Emma struggled against him in earnest, gaining little traction and succeeding in doing nothing but rubbing her belly back and forth against his rapidly hardening desire.

Jonah had to swallow a groan as her movements sent a wave of pleasure radiating from his groin. "Stop. Wiggling," he managed through gritted teeth. "I just want to talk. I have no intention of taking advantage of you in here, but if you keep grinding your hips against mine like that, we may have to make some impromptu changes to the agenda." The thought had undeniably crossed his mind, but even *he* had boundaries in the workplace. "I can tell you don't think that highly of me and my reputation with women, but I can assure you that I much prefer the king-size bed in my loft for that kind of thing."

"I don't want to talk. Or to see your king-size bed."

"I hadn't asked you to."

Emma stopped struggling and looked up at him. He could see the dim light reflecting in her eyes as they searched his face for something. Sincerity, maybe. She must've found it because eventually her body relaxed in his arms.

"Then what is it you want, Jonah?"

He couldn't very well tell her that he wanted to distract her until he could clean up his brother's mess. And in that moment, that wasn't his biggest motivation. There was something about the way she said his name that sent a fire raging through his veins and made him want to pull her close and kiss her. It was different from the run-of-the-mill lust most attractive women lured from him. It was more powerful. Potent. And it demanded he take action.

"I just want to get to know you. There's something happening here… I can't explain it, but I want to see where it goes." Jonah released her waist with one hand to reach up and caress her face. He just had to touch her, even if it earned him a slap.

Instead, he heard Emma's sharp intake of breath and decided he wasn't the only one whose plans were crumbling under the strain of their attraction to one another. "Tell me I'm crazy, but I know you feel it, too. You're just determined to fight it. Stop fighting."

"I…" Emma began to protest, but words seemed to escape her in that moment.

They escaped him, too. And words wouldn't fill the need building inside him. Jonah leaned in and pressed his lips against hers. He expected resistance, but he found none. There was only a slight hesitation, then surrender. Maybe it was the safety of the dark, but his uptight auditor melted into him instead, matching the enthusiasm of his touch.

He'd been correct in his assessment of her. Under that straitlaced veneer was a sensual female looking for an outlet. Jonah would gladly provide it.

Deepening the kiss, he let his tongue slide

across hers, drinking in the taste of spicy cinnamon. The flavor was sharp, biting him unexpectedly. He liked the surprise contrast. Emma was full of them.

She wrapped her arms around his neck, tugging her body closer to him. The darkness and the familiar feel of her in his arms roused thoughts of his butterfly again. If he didn't know better, he'd swear he was with her, in his laundry room. Without thinking, he let his right hand drift to her chest, stopping short of groping her breast, but aligning his hand where his butterfly's tattoo would be.

She must have misinterpreted his intentions because Emma instantly stiffened in his arms and jerked away from his kiss. "What the hell are we doing?" she whispered.

"Wait," he protested, the distance between them suddenly painful. Jonah let go of her to fumble for the light switch, but the instant he did, he felt her pull away and scramble for the doorknob. The door flew open, flooding the small room with light so he could see her dash away from him and down the hallway to the ladies' room.

Flopping back against the wall, Jonah ran his hand through his hair and wished away his erection. That hadn't exactly gone to plan.

So pulling her into a dark room and pinning her against him might've been the wrong tactic if he'd really just wanted to talk. And he had, at first. His body just had other plans. So had hers, but he went too far, as always. Damn.

He shook his head. Something about her just wasn't quite right. She was nervous around him. Avoided him at all costs. Refused to accept gifts or dinner dates. He'd watched her interact with other employees, and the stiff, overly polite veil dropped. She was still professional, just not militantly so.

Emma was just insistent on keeping the wall up between them. A wall that in the dark, crumbled in an instant. She'd let him in for a brief moment, then regained her senses and ran as fast as she could in the opposite direction.

For some reason, he absolutely repelled her and had since the first moment they met. He didn't understand at all. Yes, he was a force of nature when he wanted something, but he was also friendly, laid-back and fairly easy to get along with. Why would she fight something her body so clearly wanted?

Unless...

Jonah swallowed hard and looked out the door to watch Emma peek out, then dash down the hallway back to her office. Maybe his plan was too little, too late. Perhaps his enterprising accountant had already found the discrepancies in the books. If that was the case, it would explain a lot.

Who would want to date a man they were about to report to Game Town for keeping sketchy books?

Five

Jonah was forced back to his office for a teleconference after the closet incident, but he wasn't about to let that whole thing go. Either she knew about the missing money or she didn't. She liked him or she hated him. But he was going to find out the truth either way.

The next morning, he found her sitting in her temporary office. Jonah watched her silently for a few minutes as she sat hovering over her paperwork, studying it with unmatched intensity. Her nose wrinkled just slightly, a line of concentration settling in between her brows as she scrutinized every number.

Even at her desk and fully immersed in her work, her posture was not slouched over. She sat quite upright, her shoulders back, her breasts pressing insistently against her pink, silk blouse. Her brunette hair was pulled back again, a stray piece framing the curve of her face.

Without looking up, she tucked the strand behind her ear and started to make notes in a spiral notebook. She had some of the neatest penmanship he'd ever seen. Programmers were not known for their handwriting. He typed nearly everything aside from signing his name to contracts and checks. Her handwriting was precise and delicate with full, curling loops and sweeping letters. It suited her, he thought. Rigid and controlled at first glance, but inherently feminine and open if you took the time to study and understand her better.

Audit or no, Jonah was genuinely interested in Emma and it surprised him. She got under his skin and irritated him, but at the same time, she was a fascinating puzzle to try and solve. Yesterday's encounter just made it that much more intriguing. Figuring her out and breaking down her defenses would be an achievement on par with the first time he'd beaten *Legend of Zelda* as a kid.

"What's the matter, Mr. Flynn? Run out of women to abduct so you thought you'd stop by my office and try again?"

The sound of Emma's voice pulled him from his thoughts. She was watching him, but he didn't see the tension in her shoulders that was there before. There was even a touch of amusement in her voice, which surprised him. Giving her some space had been the right thing to do.

"I'm sorry about yesterday. I hadn't intended—"

"That's fine," she interrupted. "It's not a problem. Let's just pretend it never happened."

Jonah didn't expect this. He expected her to be wound tight and ready for a fight, or at least, a harassment suit. Instead, she was insistent on keeping things professional and putting it behind them. Perhaps she hadn't found Noah's indiscretion after all. "Can we talk about it?"

"I'd rather not."

A blush lit her cheeks and Emma let her gaze

drop back to her paperwork. She actually looked embarrassed. Jonah had no idea what that was about. It had been virtually impossible to make most of the women he'd dated blush, much less embarrass them with talk of romantic embraces. He wanted to see her porcelain complexion flush pink again, this time after they kissed. Kissing in the dark had robbed him of that tantalizing visual.

"Let me make it up to you."

At that, she rolled her eyes and pushed away from her desk. The sweet blush was gone. "Please…"

"…go to dinner with you? Very well, I accept. How about o ya for sushi? I haven't gotten to try there yet."

Emma stopped in her tracks, seemingly startled by his turn of the conversation. "What? No."

"No sushi? You're right. That's not everyone's cup of tea. How about a steak house?"

"No. I mean, *no*, I don't want to go to dinner." Her face blushed a deeper red this time; she was clearly flustered with irritation. She brushed past him into the hallway. He took a moment to ad-

mire the tight fit of her black pants as she saun-
tered away, then jogged a few steps to catch up
to her.

"Why not?" he asked, pulling alongside.

"It would be inappropriate," she said over her
shoulder.

"Says who? I'm not your boss. I don't see
anything wrong with taking you to dinner as a
friendly welcome to my company. I take clients
out to eat all the time."

"You haven't built a reputation like yours on
simply being *friendly* to women."

Her sharp words jabbed at Jonah. It sounded
like her concerns were less about it appearing
inappropriate to others and more about her less-
than-flattering opinion of his love life. "Ah, so
you don't want to be seen in public with a man
whore like me, right? Would it damage your
sparkling reputation, Emma?"

Emma picked up her pace, quickly turning
a corner and heading down an empty hallway,
probably to the copier again. "Honestly, yes. I've
worked very hard to get where I am. I'm not in-

terested in men like you or the kind of 'friend-
liness' you offer."

They stopped outside the elevator and she
pushed the down button, refusing to look him in
the eye. It made him wonder why. Those words
didn't jibe with the woman who had kissed him
in the dark supply closet. "I don't know..." he
teased, letting a sly smile curve his lips. "You
might like sullying your reputation a bit with me.
It didn't seem to bother you so much yesterday."

Her head snapped around to look at him with a
frown pulling down the corners of her pink lips.
"Or I might end up in one of those gossip rags
and have everyone talking about me."

Jonah hated those publications. Why anyone
was interested in his life, he didn't know. "Who
cares what other people think about what you
and I do?"

The doors opened and Emma rushed inside
with Jonah in her wake. "I care. You might be
a millionaire playboy, but I'm a professional.
Something like that could cost me my job."

"Would your boss really care about the two of
us being seen together? Why would you want

to work for someone that uptight? Come work here. I could use a new finance officer."

Emma finally looked up at him, her green eyes widening in surprise, but then shook her head. "That's a nice offer, Mr. Flynn, but I don't ever want it to be said that I earned my job on my back."

She'd called him by his formal name again. They were regressing, if that was even possible. "I never said anything about you being on your back, Emma. All I suggested was dinner. You filled in the rest based on your biased presumptions about me."

A chime announced their arrival on the next floor and she shot out the minute she could fit through the doorway. "They aren't presumptions anymore. Now they're from personal experience. Yesterday is all the proof I need to know that even something innocent can go astray when you're involved, Mr. Flynn."

That was three times now. "Please call me Jonah. Mr. Flynn is my father. And he's dead. Besides, I already apologized for that. I told you I didn't know what got into me. I won't do it again unless you ask me to. Just have dinner with me."

Emma turned suddenly and planted her hands on her hips. "Why are you dogging me so hard? Why me? Don't you have some underwear model to keep you entertained?"

Jonah shoved his hands into his pockets in frustration and made a mental note: no more models. They gave him a bad reputation and intimidated other women. He had a universal appreciation of the female body in all its forms. Women rarely understood that, though. They just measured themselves against this perfect ideal and didn't think he could desire them, as well.

"What if I truly, genuinely, was interested in you, Emma? That I thought you were smart and funny and attractive and wanted to see what could happen between us? Is that so bad?"

"In any other time and any other place, maybe not. But as it stands, no dinner. No dates. Just, no thank you." Emma turned and marched into the coffee shop.

It was fairly empty at this hour, so Jonah followed her, refusing to end this conversation until he'd won. "Let me at least buy you coffee."

Emma chuckled and crossed her arms protectively over her chest. "It's free in here."

Jonah arched a brow in amusement. "Not for me, it isn't. I pay for it all. As a matter of fact, I've bought you several meals since you've been here. What's the harm in one more? The only difference is that we eat it at the same time at the same table."

She narrowed her green gaze at him and sighed. "You're not going away until I at least agree to have coffee with you, are you?"

"Coffee is a good start."

"Fine," she said. "I'll have a tall hot tea with two sugars, one cream, and a cinnamon roll. I'll be waiting at a table. And when we're done, I don't want to see you for the rest of the day. Got it?"

Jonah grinned wide, the small victory seeming bigger when Emma was involved. "Absolutely."

He found her seated at a table in the back corner of the coffee shop a few minutes later. Jonah watched silently as she doctored her hot tea and removed the bag. "What got you into accounting?" he asked. This wasn't the time or place for bold moves or hard questions.

"I dislike ambiguity," she responded. "In math, there is no gray area, no questionable decisions. Two plus two equals four. I liked having a career based in something I could depend on. It also seemed to be a respectable profession. My parents were both pleased with my decision."

"And what if you'd wanted to be a fashion model or a rock star?" Jonah asked. "What would they have thought about that?"

Emma only shook her head. "I would never want to do something like that. For one thing, I'm not pretty enough or talented enough. And even if I were, I wouldn't do it. Those kinds of people end up in the magazines right beside you."

Jonah frowned. He didn't like the way she spoke about herself. "It's not so bad," he countered. "People read those magazines because they want to live vicariously through people like me. They want to share in the glamour and excitement."

"My sister was the one destined for the spotlight, not me."

"And what does your sister do?" Jonah asked.

"Nothing. She's dead." Emma put the lid on her cup and picked up her plate. "I'm sorry, Jonah, but I've got to get back to work."

Emma flopped back into her desk chair and buried her face in her hands. This was not going at all to plan. Before she'd come to FlynnSoft, she'd been confident that its handsome CEO wouldn't want anything to do with her. Finding out Jonah was the father of her unborn child made it even more critical that she maintain her distance until her audit was complete. There was tiny, living proof that she'd slept with the FlynnSoft CEO at least once, and that was too much. And yet in the last twenty-four hours, she'd made out with him in a dark closet and agreed to have coffee with him.

What the hell was wrong with her? Kissing Jonah? She wished she could say she lost her mind in that dark room, but what was her excuse today? Chatting with him over breakfast pastry and caffeinated drinks seemed harmless, but they both knew it was anything but. If she gave him an inch, he'd take a mile. There was no such thing as harmless where the two of them were concerned.

Despite her accusations to the contrary, she was fairly certain all Jonah had intended to do yesterday was get her somewhere private and force the conversation she was adamant to avoid. But somewhere things just went wildly off course. Again.

It was just like Mardi Gras all over again. Whatever powerful, magnetic force drew them together and lured them into a night of hedonistic pleasure was still in play. Being pressed against Jonah again, his warm, male scent teasing her brain with arousing memories... It was like the last three months without him never happened.

But they had happened. And for a reason.

The minute his hand came near her chest, the cautionary reminder of her tattoo sent a spike of panic through her. He couldn't see and didn't know he was inches from completing their tattoo, but she knew. And it was far too close for comfort. All she could do was turn and run. Like that night, she couldn't change what she'd just done, but she could put a stop to it and make sure it didn't happen again. He could be a part of her life as the father of her child, but nothing more. And not yet.

This was all her girlfriends' faults. They'd sown the seeds of doubt and discontent in her mind when they came over for dinner. Emma lay awake for hours thinking about the night she'd spent with Jonah and the lonely, miserable ones that had followed since.

She'd convinced herself that a man like Jonah would never be satisfied with a woman like her. The woman who fell into his arms that night didn't really exist. Keeping their romance anonymous was what kept it special, what made it into the fantasy she couldn't forget. It could never be ruined by the reality of who they really were, come daylight. And yet, the child they'd created that night would make destroying that fantasy a necessity.

After the last few days working with Jonah,

she was beginning to wonder if ruining the fantasy would matter to him. Inexplicably, there was a draw between them that had nothing to do with masks and secrets. He had no idea who she really was and yet Jonah Flynn seemed genuinely interested in her. He was going out of his way to get her attention and she couldn't understand why. He couldn't possibly want her as she was. She seemed to do nothing but irritate him, based on the crease that was constantly present between his eyebrows.

Was he simply trying to woo his way into a favorable audit finding? It wouldn't be the first time someone had tried to bribe or coerce an auditor. It had never happened to Emma before, so maybe she was being naive about his attentions. Perhaps a man like Jonah preferred the more pleasurable option of seducing them over laying out cash. The spark between them might simply make his job easier.

Of course, if he was going to that much trouble, it meant he had something to hide…

A deep feeling of unease pooled in Emma's stomach. This was a huge and very important contract for FlynnSoft. If he was afraid she might uncover something that could risk it, she had no doubt he'd go out of his way to distract her. He didn't necessarily have to think she was smart or pretty to pull it off. How could he, when he was used to dating fashion models and pop stars? Emma was just the rich daughter of someone far more important than she was. If all he really cared about was nailing the deal with Game Town, he would be willing to do it by any means necessary. Suspecting his motives would make it easier to ignore his advances, right?

At least for now. He'd certainly wanted her back in February when there were no audits, no accounts and no contracts. But then she wasn't herself that night.

Emma tried to push that thought aside and focus on the numbers the rest of the afternoon. While her work might seem boring to some, what she'd said to Jonah about math was true. It never lied. It was a constant, and she found working with numbers to be soothing. She could lose herself for hours in the books, and today was no different. When she looked up, it was after six. Jonah had thankfully kept his promise to stay away for the rest of the day and she'd managed to get a lot done.

She considered packing up and going home, but restlessness still plagued her. She decided she'd been sitting for too long and headed straight down to the FlynnSoft gym. She'd packed a bag of workout clothes and brought them in after the guilty tiramisu consumption.

Tonight wasn't about calories, though. She needed an outlet for the frustration and nervous energy threatening to bubble out of her, and some pounding on the elliptical machine was just the thing since pounding Jonah was not an option. She honestly wasn't sure how much of this she could take. He was relentless, absolutely aggravating and refusing to take no for an answer. Her afternoon of peace would be the exception, not the rule, she was certain. Especially now that he knew he could wear her down after a while and get his way.

It made her wonder if he knew who she really was. Maybe it wasn't about the audit at all. She hadn't found a single questionable thing in the books to warrant a distraction. And yet, it would be impossible for Jonah to recognize her from that night. Not a bit of her tattoo had seen the light of day. Their conversations offered no clues to her identity or their past. And yet he was constantly in pursuit of her.

Before she headed down to the gym, she stopped at the desk of Jonah's assistant, Pam. "Is Mr. Flynn gone for the day?" she asked.

"Yes, he had a five-thirty dinner engagement."

Perfect. "Thank you."

Emma made her way down the hall, thankful that she would be able to work out in peace. In the locker room, Emma changed quickly into her standard gym clothes, which consisted of a tank top over a sports bra and a pair of jogging shorts. The top left the tattoo partially exposed and clung to the barely rounding belly of her pregnancy, making her frown in the mirror. She hadn't thought about that when she packed her bag, but the time of baggy clothes and maternity outfits was right around the corner.

She considered changing back into her regular clothes and just heading home for the night, but she was actually looking forward to the workout. Emma glanced into the still-empty workout room and decided it was safe enough since Jonah wouldn't be around to see it. No one else would understand the significance of either the tattoo or the belly.

The coast was clear. Harper was right. Apparently, software programmers were more likely to make use of the coffee bar and pinball machine than the exercise facilities. She jumped onto the closest elliptical machine, putting her water bottle into the cup holder and plugging her earbuds into her phone to listen to her favorite workout music.

Emma selected an upbeat seventies playlist and started moving to the disco beat that thrummed through her body. She closed her eyes and gave in to it. The sweat running down her spine and the ache of her muscles were welcome distractions from the confusion and arousal that had been her constant companions the last few days. She hoped that if she worked out long enough, her attraction to Jonah would seep out her pores and she would be better prepared to deal with him.

At least that was the idea.

Emma had always been a fan of exercise. You wouldn't think it to look at her, but she recognized it as an outlet for her body's impulses. The all-girls private school she attended for high school had encouraged them to be as active as possible. The nuns insisted that sweat was purifying and there was no desire that couldn't be suppressed with a good workout.

She had reason to be a believer in its powers and fell back on it instead of eating when stress took over her life. She lost ten pounds after her breakup with David in February. Between him leaving and the fallout of her twenty-four-hour rebellion, she'd clocked in serious overtime at the gym. She'd finally regained those ten pounds due to her blossoming pregnancy, but she continued to work out, nonetheless. She didn't want to get too large and spend valuable time post-partum worrying about extra pounds instead of enjoying precious moments with her newborn.

When her body was about to give out from the strain, Emma slowed her pace to cool down and opened her eyes. She smiled, pleased with her workout stats on the console. She may well have earned herself a treat after dinner. Maybe some nice dark chocolate would provide a pseudo-sexual chemical release to back her down from the edge.

Emma silenced her music and stepped onto the padded floor with gelatinous kneecaps. Her plan had worked. She was exhausted, sticky and thirsty. Sex with Jonah was the last thing she wanted at the moment. She reached for her water, taking a healthy swig, then began wiping her face with her towel.

The sound of a man's laughter startled her. She yanked the towel from her face, pulled out her earbuds and looked around the gym, but found it to be just as empty as it had been before. Her only guess was that it must've been someone in the hallway walking past the gym. Or maybe her imagination was getting the best of her.

With another quick glance around, she gathered up her things and headed to the locker room just to be safe. Originally, she'd planned to shower and change here, but the unknown man's laughter left her unnerved. What if Jonah had seen her? She had taken a huge risk tonight and she couldn't repeat it. She needed to bring some gym clothes to work that wouldn't leave her so exposed next time. Jonah might be out tonight, but that wouldn't be the case every time she came down here.

Instead, she grabbed her tote bag, slipped a hoodie over her clothes just in case and headed to the exit.

She could bathe in private at home where she didn't have to worry about who might be watching.

Six

Jonah ducked into a corridor and watched Emma as she headed toward the back exit of the building. When his dinner meeting was canceled earlier tonight, he was already at the restaurant waiting. He opted to get a to-go order and take it back to the office. There, he planned to get in some weight training—it was legs day—and eat his dinner as he went over some emails.

The gym was usually empty in the evenings and he enjoyed the solitude. He spent all day in meetings and on phone calls. His time at the gym was an hour out of the day where he could lose himself in some music and let his sore muscles distract him from his worries. He never expected to find Emma there. She seemed like the kind of woman who didn't like to get dirty, much less sweat. Yet there she had been, going to town on one of the machines, music pumping into her ears, her eyes closed.

If he didn't know better, he'd say she was trying to work something out of her system. Perhaps he'd done a better job of sexually frustrating her than he thought. Maybe she only resisted him on the surface.

He'd almost opened his mouth to say as much to her when she suddenly came to a stop and climbed down from the machine. He watched her from the doorway, unnoticed, as she sipped her water and wiped the sweat from her flushed face. It was then that he spied a flash of red peeking out from her black top. He took a few steps farther into the gym and could clearly see half a red heart tattooed on her left breast. Jonah had stopped, looked at the tattoo on his hand, then at her tiny, rounded stomach in disbelief before choking on a nervous laugh and darting out of the gym before she saw him.

Could it be?

Never. Never in a million years would he have pegged Emma as his butterfly. His butterfly had been free, uninhibited, wild. On the surface, Emma appeared to be anything but. She'd told him she was acting out of character that night, but he didn't really believe her. Everyone said something like that when they found themselves in an awkward situation.

She must've been telling the truth. His butterfly had also told him that he wouldn't want her in the morning, like she'd turn into a pumpkin at sunrise. Instead, she turned into an uptight accountant. A beautiful, graceful, aggravating, uptight accountant who looked as though she might be carrying his child.

He was no expert in that department. What he did know was that three months ago, her belly had been flat as a board, trembling as he planted kisses across it. Emma wouldn't show much at three months, but it was hard to hide a belly in workout clothes. Could she really be having his child?

That was something Jonah had never really

considered. He wasn't opposed to children as a whole, but he'd not envisioned his life as one where he would settle down and have a family. Maybe one day, but one day always seemed a long way off. It certainly wasn't six months from now.

Jonah let his head roll back against the wall with a dull thud that did little to help the situation. A baby. Was it really possible that Emma was having his child? They'd used protection. He always used protection. He wasn't stupid. There were plenty of women who would be happy to carry his heir to inherit his money along with his blue eyes. Emma didn't seem at all like that kind of woman.

Of course, if you'd asked him an hour ago, he would've told you she was the kind of woman who would tell a man when she was having his baby. And yet she hadn't.

Jonah shook his head and started back down the hallway to his office. He couldn't work out now. His head wasn't in it. Besides, this revelation changed everything.

His pursuit of Emma had been purely business

at first. Yes, distracting her would be a pleasurable chore to cover his ass and Noah's until
the finances were cleaned up, but still business.
When she rebuffed him, it had become a challenge. He always enjoyed conquering impossible tasks.

But now it was a matter of pride. Emma knew
who he was. Had known almost from the moment they'd met. She'd seen his hand, seen his
tattoo and yet had said nothing despite the fact
that she was carrying his child.

Why? The tattoos were supposed to help
bring them together. The only link from the
night of fantasy to their reality. Seeing his tattoo should've been a sign to her, a pleasant surprise, especially since she had no other way to
contact her baby's father. If he'd found her first,
he would've instantly told her who he was. Unless she thought their night together was a mistake. Or that she didn't want him in her or their
baby's life now that she knew who he really was.

Impossible! What woman wouldn't be thrilled
to find the father of her child was secretly a rich,
successful and attractive businessman? There

were plenty of outcomes to that scenario that weren't nearly as positive.

Jonah reached his office and spied a copy of a recent entertainment magazine on Pam's desk. It was flipped open to a page that featured a picture of him with a woman he'd only gone out with once or twice. The byline read "Software playboy romances lingerie model." He frowned.

Okay, so maybe his celebrity status wasn't helping his cause. He had a reputation for being a badass and he liked it. Women were just part of the package. Most women didn't mind getting a piece of him, no matter how brief.

Emma was different. He knew that much. She wasn't the type of woman to tolerate that kind of crap from a man. She was an old-fashioned woman who expected the romantic overtures that were practically dead in this day and age. Not flowers and jewelry, but time and attention. The kind of woman who made him cringe. *Needy* and *clingy* were two adjectives that quickly axed a woman from his address book.

And yet she was also the woman who had filled the last three months with erotic fantasies he couldn't shake. The one who had occupied his thoughts and forced him to compare every other date to the high bar she'd set. So far, no one had measured up.

Pushing the door open and entering his office, he threw his exercise towel over the back of his guest chair. She'd sat in that very chair when she'd had her panic attack.

The attack that had immediately followed their shaking hands. That had to be the moment she realized who he was. Not exactly the romantic response he'd pictured in his mind when they'd sat in that tattoo parlor and held hands while getting inked.

All this time, he'd been worried that her nerves and avoidance of him had been related to the audit. That she'd found out about Noah's indiscretion already. Instead, there had been a bigger issue—she was trying to keep him from uncovering the truth about her. Apparently they both had secrets to hide.

For whatever reason, Emma wasn't interested in Jonah and didn't want him to know who she was. She'd resisted his every advance like no other woman had before, even knowing she was carrying his child. Why would she be so determined to keep that from him? Wasn't he good enough to be her baby's father? Would she prefer some quiet, unassuming banker or insurance broker who would provide stability and no passion?

He didn't believe that for a second. The woman he'd spent Mardi Gras with had been complex, with layers that included passionate minx. Sure, he had a reputation for being wild, too, but he was an adult and knew there was a time and place for everything. Being a responsible father was a duty he wouldn't shirk, no matter how low her opinion of him might be.

Their recent time together proved that she was also a strong-willed, stubborn woman who thought she could outwit him. Emma really thought she could keep this secret from him.

Jonah twisted his lips in thought as he reached for his butterfly photo. He'd imagined the moment he found her would be like taking his first breath, starting his life anew with the amazing woman he'd longed for all this time. Instead, his mystery lover thought he was nothing more than an irritating pebble in her shoe.

But she hadn't seen anything yet.

It wasn't that long ago that he'd coaxed her into a wild night of uninhibited passion and recklessness. Considering the uptight accountant he'd come to know, that was no small feat. Knowing he'd done it once, however, Jonah was confident he could do it again. Before he was done with Emma, she'd be putty in his hands, all too eager to confess her identity and fall into his arms for good.

Until then, the torture would be sweet.

Emma couldn't shake the sensation of being watched. It had been that way since the night before at the gym. Every time she felt the urge to pull her gaze away from her computer screen, she expected to see Jonah loitering in her doorway with his smug, cat-that-ate-the-canary grin. But he wasn't there. In fact, she hadn't seen or heard from him since the coffee shop encounter the day before.

She knew better than to let her guard down,

however. She'd made that mistake last night and couldn't do it again.

More importantly, Emma needed to focus on the books. Something wasn't adding up right and unless she could shut down every part of her brain but the one that dealt with numbers, she'd never be able to determine if this was a real issue or one caused by her own distraction.

The third time she tried running through it and got the same result, she sat back in her chair with a groan. She'd obviously made a mistake a few pages back. A huge chunk of money was missing. "Damn it," she cursed, pushing the unruly strand of hair from her face for the twentieth time today. She needed to buy a barrette.

"What's the matter, Miss Dempsey?"

Startled, Emma sat bolt upright in her seat and clutched her hand to her chest. As she looked over this time, Jonah was loitering in her doorway when she'd least expected him.

"Nothing," she insisted. Even if she had found something of concern in the financials, she wouldn't mention it to anyone until she was absolutely certain. You didn't pull the fire alarm until you saw the flames. Right now, this was just a little smoke. No one was stupid enough to do something that obvious. Smart people took money in small chunks. There had to be an explanation.

She took a deep breath to steady herself and looked back up at Jonah. There was something different about the way he carried himself today. Emma couldn't quite put her finger on it, exactly, but something had changed. Perhaps it was the sly twist of his full lips and the knowing twinkle in his eye. She had no idea what would have pleased him so greatly this afternoon, so she chose to ignore it and the deep-down pangs of desire it caused inside of her.

"Well, I just got off the phone with your boss."

At the mention of her supervisor, the desire immediately melted away like an ice cube dropped into boiling water. "You spoke with Tim? Is there a problem?"

Jonah shook his head. "No, not at all. He was just calling to see if you had settled in okay."

Emma held her breath as she listened to his response. Tim never just called to see if an employee was settled in. He didn't care that much. Knowing him, Tim was calling to see if Emma had fallen for Jonah's charms yet. "And what did you tell him?"

Jonah pursed his lips for a second, drawing out her torture with obvious pleasure. "I told him that you were the most polite and professional worker in the building, myself included. Why? What did you think I would say?"

Emma shrugged. "I don't know," she admitted. "Hopefully nothing related to the supply closet."

At that, he chuckled and gripped the door frame of her office, flashing his tattoo at her. "I didn't build a successful company by being a fool, Emma. And despite what you seem to think, I'm not out to put your job in jeopardy."

She expelled a sigh of relief that was premature.

"It did occur to me," he continued, "that your boss seemed like a bit of a hard-ass. I get why you're so concerned about appearances. And that's why I'm offering you a compromise."

Emma tried not to frown. There was nothing to compromise over.

"You don't want to be seen with me because it's inappropriate. I get that. But I am going to take you to dinner one way or another. So I can either find a way to blackmail you into having dinner with me here in town, or you can accept my offer of having dinner with me out of town, where no one will find out."

Blackmail? Emma leaped up from her chair. "I don't know what the hell you're playing at, Jonah, but there's nothing to blackmail me with."

He didn't seem fazed by her sudden bravado. "So you say. And maybe that's true. But there's nothing stopping me from telling Tim some fabricated misdeed. He'll believe me over you, don't you think?"

Emma's jaw dropped. "You wouldn't. Why would you even consider such a thing?"

Jonah crossed his arms over his chest, wrinkling the fabric of his flannel shirt. "Because I get what I want, Emma. And I want you to have dinner with me. If I thought for one second that you weren't sincerely interested, I would let it drop. But you can't fool me with your tight hair buns and your formal demeanor. The woman that was in the supply closet with me wants to have dinner. And who am I to deny her?"

"You don't know anything about me, in or out of a closet, Jonah."

"Don't I?"

His blue eyes challenged her, and that made her instantly nervous. She self-consciously reached for the collar of her blouse and pulled it tighter to ensure she hadn't given away her identity.

"I certainly don't want to take it this far, which is why I'm offering you an alternative that will make everyone happy. Tomorrow night, meet me at the Wall Street Heliport at six sharp. From there, I will whisk you away to a location where we won't run into anyone we know. We can have a nice, private dinner without you needing to worry about your job. You can just relax for once and enjoy your time with me."

It wasn't an ideal scenario, but it was certainly better than losing her job over a lie. She couldn't believe a man that high profile could just disappear like that, though. "And what about your little paparazzi friends?"

Jonah shrugged. "They only take pictures

when I allow them to know where I am. When I want privacy I'm more than capable of arranging it. I assure you that no one will know where we're going tomorrow night, even you."

That was one less concern, but it still left several on the table she wasn't ready to discuss with him. Like how being alone with him turned her knees to butter and how if she fell prey to his charms, she'd run the risk of him finding out all her secrets. It was too soon for that. But did she really have a choice? "And if I go to dinner with you…just dinner…you'll leave me alone?"

"If at the end of the evening that's what you want, then yes."

Emma would make sure that was how the evening ended, even if she regretted every word out of her mouth. While she didn't anticipate much to come out of her attraction to the infamous CEO, she didn't want even a whisper of it to happen before her job here was completed.

"Okay, fine," she said in a huge rush of breath before she could change her mind. "What shall I wear?"

Jonah grinned wide with unmasked pleasure.

"Excellent. Now you might be surprised to hear this, but I plan to take you somewhere that requires a jacket and maybe even a tie on my part."

Emma's eyebrows shot up in surprise. "You mean you own a suit?"

"I own several. I'm not antisuit under the right circumstances, despite what my mother would say if she were asked. I just don't need them to feel important or in control like some people do. I like to be comfortable and a T-shirt with a video game reference on it is far more representative of my personality than a boring old pin-striped tie."

Emma tried not to get excited by the idea of seeing Jonah in a suit. He obviously underestimated what a sharp suit on the right man could do to a woman's resolve. "Then I'll meet you at the heliport tomorrow at six."

Jonah gave her a curt nod and disappeared from her office. Once he was gone, Emma was finally able to take a deep breath and realized what she'd just agreed to. She peeked out around her door, and when he was nowhere in sight, dashed down the hallway to Harper's cubicle.

"Help!" she said as she rounded the corner.

Harper looked up with wide, surprised eyes. "What's the matter?"

"I've got a date tomorrow. With *him*."

"Him?" Harper leaped up from her chair. "I thought you refused to go out with him right now."

"I know, but he shot down every excuse I could think of. I agreed to it this time on the condition that he would leave me alone after that if I asked him to."

Harper just shook her head. "How could you ever ask a man like him to leave you alone?"

"Well," Emma sighed, "at the moment, I have bigger problems than that."

"Like what?"

"Like I have no idea what I'm going to wear. Most of my clothes are somewhere between business casual and business professional. I need date clothes. You're the fashion diva. I need you to go through my closet and tell me what to wear."

"I doubt there's much in there we can use," Harper said with obvious dismay. "Especially with junior playing havoc with your waistline. I think we need to go shopping."

Emma frowned. "I don't think I have time to—"

"Right now," Harper interrupted. She reached into her desk drawer and pulled out her Kate Spade purse. "Get your things. We're going shopping right now."

Emma let Harper shove her down the hallway as she protested. "It's three in the afternoon."

"You need all the help you can get."

Emma couldn't argue with that. The next thing she knew they were in a cab and on their way to Fifth Avenue. As they strolled along the sidewalk, Harper had her gaze narrowed at every window scanning for just the right thing. They had stepped into about seven or eight stores, but left with nothing. Harper was searching for something special—a standout look—she said.

Emma was happy to hang back and let Harper decide what was best. After all, that was what Harper lived for—designer clothes, cute shoes, a fabulous handbag—she didn't need much else in life. Her apartment was paid for, so Emma was pretty sure that her entire paycheck from FlynnSoft went directly to Neiman Marcus or Saks Fifth Avenue. Thankfully, she was raised by a father with more money than he, or she, could ever spend.

And that was coming from Emma's point of view—a girl who'd never wanted for a thing in her life.

"That!" Harper came to a sudden stop and pointed at a mannequin in the window. "That's what you're wearing." She snatched Emma's hand and pulled her into the boutique before she had really even gotten a good look at the dress. All she saw was a blur of blue.

When they stopped at the rack inside the store, Emma realized it wasn't even a dress. It was a jumpsuit. "Are you serious?"

"Absolutely. Jumpsuits are very in right now. Any woman he's dated could wear some slinky little dress to dinner. That's what he expects. Blow him out of the water with this instead."

Harper held up the royal blue silk jumpsuit and Emma's eyes got big. It was sleeveless with wide

straps that went over the shoulders and a neckline that dipped down to her sternum. She'd need
a specialty bra to pull this outfit off, for sure.

"What about my tattoo?" Emma whispered.

"It will cover it. The wide straps are perfect."

That was one concern dealt with. "And where's
the back of it?" she asked.

"The fabric crisscrosses in the back and leaves
the rest bare. Just enough skin to be sexy, but
not overtly so. Pair it with some silver heels and
a silver chain belt and you're going to look fabulous. Ooh…maybe even a chunky bracelet."

Emma frowned at the dress—*er*—jumpsuit.
She wasn't ready to talk about accessories yet.
She'd never even worn a jumpsuit before. She
wasn't entirely sure she could pull it off. Then
again, it would make it easier to get in and out
of the helicopter if she wasn't worried about her
dress blowing up over her head. She could appreciate the practicality of that.

"So what do you think?" Harper pressed.

It was also the same blue as his eyes. She could
almost feel his warm hand brushing against the
bare small of her back as he escorted her into

a restaurant. It sent a chill through her whole body and she finally came to appreciate Harper's genius.

"I think we need to try it on."

Seven

Emma anxiously stepped out of her cab outside the Wall Street Heliport. Before she headed inside, she made certain to adjust her jumpsuit and ensure everything was in place. It was all fine. She looked amazing in the jumpsuit, something she never would've believed until she looked in the mirror at the store and noticed her jaw had dropped along with Harper's.

She took a deep breath, swung her uncharacteristically loose brunette waves over her shoulder and headed inside. Looking around the small waiting room, she didn't see Jonah anywhere at first. Only a few of the seats were taken, mostly with families awaiting helicopter tours around Manhattan. Then she noticed a tall, slim man in a dark gray suit at the window with his back to her. Could it be?

As though he sensed her arrival, the man turned around to look at her, and she was surprised to see it *was* Jonah standing there. He was wearing a royal blue dress shirt, almost the same shade as her jumpsuit, but it was unbuttoned at the collar, with no tie in sight. Even then, the effect was amazing. The suit coat highlighted his broad shoulders and the narrow hips she remembered cradling between her thighs. The blue of the shirt made his eyes an even deeper shade, like the darkest waters of the ocean.

Standing there with his hands casually stuffed into his pants pockets, he looked every inch the powerful CEO of a software empire. And yet, he had been right about it being an unnecessary accessory. He didn't need an expensive suit to command the attention of every person in the room. The crisp lines and exquisite tailoring on his body were just the delicious icing on the man cake that made her heart race in her chest and her resolve weaken.

Emma had to remind herself that although this felt like a date, it wasn't really. He didn't know who she was and she couldn't be certain of his motives for asking her out. Besides, being black-mailed into dinner was not a date. And yet she couldn't help preening as he took his turn look-ing her over from head to toe. She went with it, ignoring everyone else in the waiting area and giving him a little spin to showcase the bare back and the fit that clung to her curves. If he was a little uncomfortable all night, all the bet-ter.

His pleased smirk convinced her it was the right choice of outfit for the evening. When he was finished admiring her, she approached the window and closed the gap between them. "Good evening, Mr. Flynn."

"Tonight, of all nights," he insisted, "it's Jonah. You can call me Mr. Flynn at work tomorrow if you insist."

"I suppose that depends on how tonight goes," she added with a smile, and then turned to look at the helicopters waiting just outside. "So when will our ride be ready?"

"It's ready now." Jonah turned to the desk and gestured to the man at the counter. The attendant buzzed them out and Jonah pushed open the door that led to the helipad. "Just waiting on you."

Stepping outside, she was glad it was a calm day, not too windy. Emma had been in a helicopter twice with her parents. Sometimes her father needed to be able to get back from the Hamptons for a work emergency faster than a car or train would allow. It had never been her favorite mode of travel, but the unsteady movement didn't bother her, thankfully. Even so, she was sucking on a ginger candy to soothe her stomach just in case. She would not be remembered by Jonah as the woman who puked in the helicopter.

As they approached the sleek black helicopter, the pilot waved to them. He and Jonah helped her up inside and once she was buckled in, Jonah climbed in beside her and shut the door.

"Where are we going to dinner?" she asked as the blades started to spin overhead.

"It's a surprise."

"Of course it is," Emma muttered, but her voice was drowned out by the sound of the helicopter.

Jonah offered her a headset to wear and she accepted it. It muffled the engine sounds and allowed her to speak to the others without shouting. She didn't have much to say at first. It was a clear day and she was too busy admiring her city. New York by helicopter was a truly amazing sight. You could get up close to the architectural wonders, unlike taking a plane, and without getting bogged down by the traffic and the noise of being on the ground.

She thought they might be heading toward Long Island, but then the helicopter turned and headed farther north. They could be heading to Boston, perhaps. Or Martha's Vineyard. It was high season there.

"Stop trying to guess," Jonah said to her through the headsets. "I can see it all over your face. You're not going to be right and it will make you crazy trying to figure it out. Just relax and enjoy the flight."

Emma smirked and flopped back against her seat. She supposed he was right. Instead of looking for clues, she glanced out the window to take in the view. When she turned back to Jonah a few minutes later, she noticed he was intently watching her instead of the landscape speeding by.

"I suppose the view bores you when you've seen it repeatedly."

"Not at all," he said. "I've just got something more intriguing to look at this time."

Emma gasped softly, but didn't know what to say. Instinctively, she held her breath as he leaned close to her and put his arm around her shoulder. She started to worry that he would be able to see down her top from this angle, but it was hard to focus on that when she could smell his cologne and feel the warm press of his leg against hers.

"Thank you for agreeing to have dinner with me."

"You didn't really give me a choice," she replied, mostly in jest.

Jonah only shrugged. "I know. And I apologize for that. I guess I just wasn't sure what to do when you kept turning me down."

"Taking the hint was always an option."

"Yes." He laughed. "And I would have if your eyes were sending the same message as your mouth. But I could see you were conflicted, so I thought I'd give you a little push in the right direction."

"Threatening to get me fired is not a little push. That's blackmail."

Jonah winced. "Agreed. It was a drastic step on my part. But I wouldn't have called your boss, for the record. I was bluffing."

Emma crossed her arms over her chest, realizing too late that it gave him a tantalizing view of her cleavage. His blue eyes flickered down for only a moment before returning to hers. She was surprised by his restraint.

"Even if you're mad at me, by the end of the night, we will have kissed and made up," he said confidently.

Emma couldn't help but arch an eyebrow at

him. "You're just used to getting your way, aren't you?"

"Usually."

She eyed the full swell of his bottom lip as he spoke, remembering those lips as they sucked salt and lime juice from her body at the Mardi Gras party. The memory sent a flush of heat to her cheeks that she was certain he could see. She turned away from him, looking out as the sun started to set and lights began twinkling in the distance.

"Perhaps not this time," she said, both hoping she was right and knowing she was wrong. Every minute she spent with Jonah, the more convinced she was that she wouldn't be able to resist him much longer.

"Mr. Flynn, we're about five minutes from landing."

Jonah smiled and pulled away from her. "Excellent. See, now it didn't take very long to get here, did it?"

Emma glanced at her phone in her purse. It had been a little over forty minutes. Not far enough for Boston. Too far for the Hamptons. She didn't recognize the skyline, but it was a smaller town on the water. She could see the shore. Within minutes, they came to a gentle, bouncing landing on top of a bank building.

"We're going to a bank?"

"Very funny. I'm actually friends with the president of this bank. He's the only one that uses the helipad and said we were welcome to make use of it tonight. It's that or fly all the way to the outskirts of town to the airport and charter a car to drive us right back here. This way we're only a block from the restaurant."

They slipped off their headsets and unfastened their seat belts. The pilot opened the door of the cabin and they stepped out onto the tarmac. "I'll be waiting on you, sir," he said.

"Thank you," Jonah replied before taking Emma's hand and leading her to the rooftop door. They took the elevator down to the lobby and exited onto a quiet street in a quaint-looking seaside village she didn't recognize.

They walked about a block before she saw a taxi go by advertising a place that claimed to have the finest seafood in Newport. Newport,

Rhode Island? She'd never been there before, although she knew it had once been a very popular summer retreat for the wealthy of New England. It was famous for its huge mansions only blocks from the sea.

Emma kept her suspicions to herself until they reached a building just off the harbor that looked like an old Georgian-style inn with white siding, dormer windows and the charm of an old-fashioned seaport village. The sign hanging overhead read Restaurant Bouchard & Inn.

"Here we are," Jonah announced as they climbed the short staircase that led inside. "The best French restaurant I've found on this side of the Atlantic."

The maître d' greeted them, noted their arrival in his book and escorted them to a table beside one of the large bay windows. Once they were alone with their menus of the day, Jonah leaned across the table. "Anything you order here will be amazingly delicious and beautiful. Their chef makes food into art. Tasty art at that."

Emma scanned the menu, desperately hoping her three years of high school French would assist her in not sounding foolish tonight when she ordered. Madame Colette would be so disappointed in her for mangling such a beautiful language. She had finally decided on a ratatouille ravioli starter and the rosemary lamb chops when the sommelier arrived at the table.

"Wine?" Jonah asked with a pointed look.

Emma was about to request a dry red to go with the lamb when she realized she wasn't allowed to drink. The last week of her life had been so different it was easy to forget about her situation. "None for me, please. I'd just like some seltzer with a twist of lime."

Jonah ordered a single glass of cabernet for himself. When the waiter came to take their order a few minutes later, she made her selections and he opted for the stuffed lobster starter and the sautéed duck breast with brandied balsamic glaze.

Emma was surprised by his flawless French accent as he ordered. As the waiter stepped away, Jonah turned to her with a mildly amused expression on his face. "What? Do you think that just because I wear jeans every day and play video games for a living that I wasn't properly educated in expensive British preparatory schools like most ridiculously rich kids?"

Emma frowned and looked down at the glass of seltzer in front of her. She was bad at making presumptions where he was concerned. He was just so different from what she was used to. It made her wish she did have wine to drown her embarrassment. "No, I'm just a little surprised—and jealous—of how flawless your accent is."

"You should hear my Japanese."

She looked back up, truly stunned this time. "You speak Japanese?"

"If you want to be successful in the Japanese video game market, you have to. I also speak Spanish and I'm learning Mandarin as we expand further into the Asian markets. I'm an accomplished pianist and was the captain of my rowing team at Harvard, although that was just to appease my parents. I would've much rather been indoors playing games or romancing the ladies. As you can see, there's a lot more to me than meets the eye, Emma. The same could be said of you."

"What do you mean?" she asked, feeling suddenly anxious at the turn of their discussion. "I'm just boring, uptight Emma the accountant."

"You're selling yourself short. For starters, you're great at keeping secrets."

Emma stiffened in her seat and swallowed hard. "Secrets? I don't—"

Jonah raised his hand to silence her protests. "Now that we're away from New York and the prying eyes of anyone that might care besides the two of us, I can say as much. And you can finally be truthful with me. Because you've known. All this time, you've known who I was and you didn't say anything to me about it."

The steely edge in Jonah's voice sent her spine straight in a defensive posture. When she looked into his eyes, however, she didn't see the anger she expected. Just hurt. The jovial, carefree CEO had a tender spot and she'd managed to find it without trying.

"We had something special and you don't seem to care about it at all. Why didn't you tell me the moment you realized who I was?" He slipped his hand, palm down, across the white linen tablecloth to expose his half of the tattoo, then wrapped his fingers around her hand.

It was happening. The moment she'd been dreading since he walked into his office and turned her world upside down. "I couldn't," she said in a hushed whisper.

"You absolutely could! You've had dozens of opportunities to speak up."

"No." Emma pulled her hand away into her lap and sat back to regain some of her personal space. "Up until this moment, we weren't just Emma and Jonah, we were the Game Town auditor and the CEO of FlynnSoft. Yes, I knew the moment I shook your hand, but I wasn't sure what to do. I know it's hard for you to understand, but I wanted to do my job first. I've been doing my damnedest to finish this audit, despite your constant distractions, so I could put it behind me and finally come to you and tell you the truth about everything."

Jonah nodded, acknowledging her struggle. "You mean about the baby."

Emma's green eyes widened in panic and Jonah felt his own pulse speed up in his throat.

She wasn't expecting him to say that at all. He'd uncovered all her secrets, it seemed.

"How did you…?" She shook her head in denial.

"I saw you in the gym the other night after work."

She continued to shake her head, letting her gaze drop to her lap. "I knew I heard someone as I was leaving. It was stupid of me to wear that outfit, but I didn't even think about it as I packed it. No one was around and I've really just started to show recently, so I didn't think anyone would notice. Especially you. You were supposed to be out at dinner." She glanced up with an accusing look in her eye.

Jonah felt his chest tighten more and more the longer she spoke. Not because of her pointed look, but because up until this moment, the baby had been a suspicion, not a fact. Yes, she skipped the wine, but she could just not like it. Yes, she had a little tummy, but she could've overindulged. He was no expert where pregnant women were concerned.

Now it was confirmed.

He was going to be a father. *A father.* He'd taken every precaution, and yet fate had laughed in his face and put him in this position anyway. He reached out to brace his hand on the edge of the table and squeezed his eyes shut. "My dinner meeting got canceled, so I came back to lift some weights. I'm usually alone in there. And yes, I sure as hell noticed. I noticed the tattoo and I noticed the…stomach. I wasn't sure until now, but I noticed."

Emma slumped back against her seat and dropped her face into her hand. "This wasn't how I wanted you to find out, Jonah. I'm sorry. I wasn't keeping it from you forever. I was going to tell you."

Jonah's head snapped up and his gaze pinned hers. "Were you?" He wasn't so sure. Sometimes she looked at him as though he were something stuck to her shoe, not the father of her child.

"I swear I was. Like I said, I wanted to finish the audit, do my job without any whispers of impropriety, but then yes, I was going to tell you who I am and that I'm pregnant. If I'd known how to contact you two months ago, I would've done it then, but by the time I figured it out, I was already involved in the audit. That said, I've been scared to death to tell you the truth."

Jonah swallowed hard and furrowed his brow. He was far from a hulking, intimidating person that people were scared of. He picked up his glass of wine and took a large sip to slow his spinning brain. "Why?"

Emma pulled her gaze from his and crossed her arms protectively over her chest. "It's like I told you that night—I'm not the woman you think I am. I knew that you wanted *her*, the wild and passionate anonymous stranger, not me. I couldn't bear to see the look on your face when you realized that I was that girl and the fantasy was shattered forever. I'm just boring old, stick-in-the-mud Emma. And to make matters worse, then I'd have to tell you that we were stuck together for the sake of our baby."

"Stuck together?" Jonah flinched at her choice of words. Is that how she saw her situation? She was *stuck* with him because they screwed up and she got pregnant?

The waiter returned with imperfect timing,

placing each of their appetizers in front of them and disappearing silently when he sensed the tension between them.

"You know what I mean!" Emma leaned in and whispered harshly across the table at him. "Even if you were disappointed beyond belief to find out it was me, even if you never wanted to lay another hand on me again, I'm having your child, Jonah. I would hope that you would want to be a part of his or her life, even if I'm just on the periphery."

Jonah didn't know what to say. He honestly didn't know how he wanted to move forward where Emma and the baby were concerned. His thoughts were spinning too quickly to light on one in particular. His strict upbringing nagged at him to marry her on the spot. Mother would insist when she found out. Noah could embezzle three million dollars, but it would be Jonah's scandal of an out-of-wedlock child that would be the biggest family disgrace in her eyes. Emma wasn't the only one constantly worried about gossip.

At the same time, his rebellious nature insisted

that people didn't get married in this day and age just because they were having a baby. He and Emma hardly knew each other, much less loved each other. Coparenting was a more popular thing for people who didn't want to make the previous generations' mistakes and stick out a miserable marriage for the sake of the children.

What did he want? Jonah had no idea. He'd barely become accustomed to the concept of fatherhood, but he certainly never imagined that Emma would just be on the periphery, no matter the scenario.

"Emma…to start off, you're not a disappointment. Look at me," he demanded, and then reached across the table and took her hand, gripping tightly so she couldn't pull away from him again. Once she reluctantly met his gaze with her own, he continued. "I mean it. While this is all a surprise, I can assure you that disappointment has never crossed my mind."

She studied his face with disbelief lining her weary eyes. How had he not noticed how tired she looked? He'd been blinded tonight by flawless makeup and the silky jumpsuit he wanted to run his hands over. Now that he was really looking, he could see the sense of overwhelming stress and exhaustion in her eyes. She was working too much, and too hard, in her condition. They'd discuss that before long.

"But I'm not the woman you wanted, Jonah. I'm not wild and sexually adventurous. I'd never done body shots or had a one-night stand before. I'd certainly never have a tattoo if it weren't for that night. Everything you saw and liked about me was out of character. I mean, I...I don't even know what I'm doing here. Coming with you tonight was a mistake."

Emma moved fast, slipping out of the booth and taking the nearest door out to the back patio that overlooked the water.

"Emma?" Jonah rushed after her, catching her wrist as she leaned over the railing seemingly looking for an escape. What was she going to do? Swim away from him? All the way back to New York?

"Emma! Would you just stop and listen to me?" he demanded as she tugged at his grip. She finally turned around to face him, leaning her back against the railing. He instinctively wrapped his arms around her waist. He knew immediately that pressing against each other like this wasn't the best idea to keep his focus, but at the very least, he could convince her that he was attracted to her.

"Jonah, I want to go home."

"If that's what you want, I will, but not until you hear me out. I sat there and listened to all your excuses for lying to me. You owe me the opportunity to tell you how I feel, whether you believe me or not."

Emma finally stilled in his arms, although her gaze was fixed on the buttons of his shirt. He breathed a sigh of relief that he could finally focus his thoughts on telling her how he felt. This was important.

"I want you to know that you're totally and completely wrong." Jonah pulled aside the blue silk strap of her jumpsuit to expose her shoulder and upper chest. He placed his hand over the curve of her breast as he'd done that first night. Their tattoos aligned, creating one heart again at last. Emma looked down at the heart with tears shimmering in her eyes, but she didn't say anything.

"These tattoos weren't just something I suggested on a whim, Emma. They were supposed to be instruments of fate. This heart becoming whole again would only happen if it was meant to. Yes, we don't know much about each other, but now is our second chance to make that happen. Not just because of the baby, but because we've been brought together again to do just that."

"Jonah…" she started to argue.

"No," he silenced her. "From the moment I saw you sitting in my office, I've had this pull towards you that I couldn't explain. It was the same feeling that led me to rescue a pretty stranger from a creep at a party. I didn't know why then and I don't know why now, but I know I'm not letting this second chance slip between our fingers. I don't know how it's going to end. No one ever does. This might not be forever. It might not turn into the love affair of the century. But we owe it to ourselves, and to our child, to at least try and see where it can take us."

She sighed and relaxed into his touch. "And what if my company finds out? I'll lose my job. They'll never believe that I can be impartial. I have a vested interest in the successful business dealings of my baby's father."

Her mention of the audit was enough to remind Jonah of why he started romancing his auditor to begin with. Yes, he'd been drawn to her, but he'd stuck it out to cover Noah's ass and keep from botching the Game Town deal. He hadn't heard from his accountant in days, and that wasn't good. Sooner or later, she was going to find the discrepancy. If he couldn't keep it from her, there was a part of him that hoped maybe she wouldn't mention it in her report as a favor to him. That he could explain it away somehow.

"Can you be impartial, Emma?" he asked.

Her green eyes met his with a hard glint shining in them. Her spine straightened and her pointed chin thrust forward in the defiant response he seemed to coax out of her so easily. "Yes. Despite what Tim thinks, I'm first and foremost a professional and I will do my job."

Jonah didn't doubt that at all. That's exactly what he was afraid of. But for now, he needed to salvage tonight and worry about Noah's mess tomorrow. "Then there's nothing your boss could say or do to prove otherwise. Now come back inside and eat that amazing-looking dinner with me."

Emma sighed and nodded. She slipped the strap of her jumpsuit back over her shoulder, hiding away the tattoo and removing the temptation of her bare skin.

They went back inside, crisis averted, and yet Jonah couldn't help but feel a new sense of worry. The audit for Game Town was at risk and it had nothing to do with Emma and everything to do with Jonah.

Eight

Thankfully, the rest of the dinner went well. Jonah had been worried that the whole evening would be ruined, but the opposite turned out to be true. Uptight Emma seemed to finally, truly relax. All her secrets were out in the open and lifting that burden had an almost-physical impact on her. She smiled more, flirted happily through dinner by sharing bites of her food and making eyes at him, and didn't once refer to him as Mr. Flynn.

All their issues weren't behind them, but they were able to at least focus on enjoying each other's company tonight and worrying about the rest tomorrow. With that thought in mind, Jonah directed the pilot to land on his building's rooftop instead of returning them to the heliport.

When they touched down, Emma frowned out the window. "Where are we?"

"My place." He opened the helicopter door and offered his hand to help her.

Suspicion wrinkled her nose, but she still accepted his hand and stepped out onto his rooftop with him. They hustled away from the helicopter and over to the door. He led her down a set of stairs and out onto the landing where the entrance to his penthouse loft was located.

"Wait a minute," Emma said as she stared at the door.

"What?"

"This was your place? Where the Mardi Gras party was held?"

"Yes," he replied as he reached out to unlock the door. Jonah didn't hold many parties at his loft in Tribeca, but the Mardi Gras shindig had been one of them. "You don't think I'm tacky enough to seduce a woman in someone else's laundry room, do you?"

Emma's cheeks flushed bright red at the mention of their impulsive encounter. "I didn't really think about it. Although now that you mention it, I think Harper did say that party was at her boss's place. I assumed she meant the head of finance, not the CEO's apartment."

"I was right under your nose the whole time," Jonah said. He pushed open the door and gestured her in ahead of him. He followed behind, watching her as she studied the open, industrial space he'd fallen in love with the first time he toured it.

"It looks different without a hundred people crammed in here. It's huge."

"It takes up the whole top floor," Jonah explained. "Originally, I think this building was some sort of textile factory. When I bought it ten years ago, part of it had been converted to offices and shops and the top two floors were a storage warehouse. I ended up turning the whole thing into loft apartments with shared common areas on the ground floor."

Emma stopped and turned to face him. "You own the whole building?"

Jonah nodded and slipped out of the suit coat that had been irritating him all evening. He was hot-blooded and the suit on top of the long-sleeved shirt and glasses of wine had him almost at the point of sweating.

"If I listened to nothing else my mother, the great Angelica Flynn, told me, I did learn to diversify my investments." He tossed the jacket over the back of a dining room chair and spread his arms out. "This was my foray into the real estate market. She thought I was crazy, of course. She prefers stuffy uptown mansions with marble and gold inlay. I like exposed brick and ductwork. Fortunately, I'm not the only one. The other lofts were rented with an extensive waiting list within weeks of being on the market."

Emma set her purse on the concrete countertop of his kitchen and ran her fingers across the slightly roughened surface. "It's definitely a different style. Not my style, but I know plenty of people who would like it."

He followed behind her as she strolled through the living room and dining area, nearing the door that led into the infamous laundry room.

As a true loft, there were only three doors in the whole space. One for the laundry and utility room, and the others for the guest and master bathrooms. Even if he'd wanted to take her to his bed that night, he wouldn't have been able to. The space was wide-open to the party. It wasn't ideal but the laundry room had been his only real option.

Emma hesitated for a moment, then reached out and turned the knob of the door. Was she really heading straight for the scene of the crime? He'd brought her back to his place with the intention of tasting every inch of her skin, but he'd anticipated using the bed this time.

She went straight to the washing machine, running her hand over the same top that he'd lifted her onto. Emma turned and pressed her back against the machine, then looked up at him with a sly smile curling her lips. "That night was…"

Mind-blowing? Crazy? Amazing? Passionate? Life changing?

"…unforgettable."

Jonah took a step closer, narrowing the gap between them. "That it was. Every minute I spent with you was seared into my brain. Every soft moan and cry permanently etched into my memory."

Emma made a familiar sound, barely louder than an intake of breath. He remembered that gasp. She'd made that same sound of surprise when he pushed up her skirt and pressed his fingertips into the flesh of her upper thighs.

He moved closer with that thought in mind. His every nerve tingled in anticipation as they remembered that moment. His blood rushed through his veins as his heart pounded loudly in his ears. "Over these last few months, I've thought of little else but having my butterfly back in my arms again."

Emma looked up at him as he came near enough to slip his arms around her waist. For once, she didn't fight or squirm. Instead, she pressed into him and clutched at the fabric of his dress shirt. "I've thought about that night a lot, too. I've wondered what I would do if I were given a second chance to be with my hero."

"Any ideas?" Jonah asked with a wicked grin. He leaned into her, pressing her back against the washing machine and imprinting his desire for her against her stomach.

"I have a few." Emma laced her fingers behind his neck and pulled his mouth down to hers.

As their lips made contact, Jonah realized this was the first time that he'd kissed Emma knowing who she really was. The kiss they'd shared before, aside from being slightly antagonistic, was just a kiss from the uptight Game Town auditor. There were no real expectations there, unlike a kiss from his butterfly.

He worried that this moment might be tainted by shaded memories of that night that no mortal woman could ever live up to. The minute they touched, however, it was no longer a concern. Her scent, her taste, the feel of her in his arms—it all combined in a familiar tidal wave that washed over him all at once. Before, there had been things about her that seemed familiar, but it had been like a déjà vu moment with one piece missing, the piece to tie it all together.

Now he had the tattoo to bring it all into focus and suddenly everything was right in the world.

He pulled her tight against him, loving the feel

of her silken tongue as it glided along his own. Her touches weren't as bold as they had been that night, but tequila did that to a person. Yes, it made her wild and uninhibited, but with her in his arms again, he realized that wasn't the part of her that he craved. Emma was wrong to think that he wouldn't want her the way she was. Who she was, was the core of what he was after. The inner woman; the one who felt free to be herself for the first time in her life.

Jonah's hands spanned her hips and he slid one up the soft fabric of her jumpsuit to caress her breast. He took advantage of the low neckline to slip his hand beneath the cups of her strapless bra and happily mold her flesh in his palm until the peaks of her nipples dug into him.

He'd never gotten to see what her breasts looked like. If he had one regret about the night they'd spent together, it was that he'd had to rush things. It wasn't the time or the place for a leisurely exploration of a woman's body. Most of their clothes stayed on in the process.

That was not going to be the case tonight.

Taking a step back, he drew in a lungful of

cool air. He braced his hands on the washing machine, trapping her there while he took a moment to collect himself.

"What's the matter?" she asked softly.

"Not a damn thing." And it was true.

"Then why—"

Jonah shook his head, interrupting her question. When he looked in her eyes, he saw confusion and disappointment mixed into the emerald green. Did she honestly think he was pulling away because he didn't want her? Nothing was further from the truth.

"Emma, I am not about to take you on this washing machine a second time. Tonight, I'm going to take my time and do it properly. I'm going to strip you naked from head to toe and press my mouth against every inch of your skin. I plan to make your body quiver and your throat go raw. So, nothing is the matter. I'm just taking a moment to keep myself from ruining my plans for tonight."

"They're good plans," she replied, and let her pink tongue snake across her bottom lip. Easing up from the washing machine, she laced her fingers behind his neck and pulled him close to her again. "You should show me where your bed is so we can implement them immediately."

Any anxiety Emma felt about this moment with Jonah vanished when he looked at her like that. He gazed at her so intently she couldn't help but believe he would do everything he promised, and then some. That was the look of a man who kept his word, and she couldn't wait.

He'd taken her hand and led her out of the laundry room and back into the main part of the loft. There, to her right, she saw the bed. Without all the party guests to block the view, it was easy to see the massive king-size bed along the far back wall of the loft.

It was placed in a niche between the bathroom and the closet to give it a little privacy despite it being out in the open. The plush, black velvet headboard rested against a wall of exposed, worn red brick. The comforter, like so much else in the loft, was a soft, steely gray that almost looked like liquid mercury pouring across the bed.

She couldn't take her eyes off their final destination. This was the moment she'd fantasized about, feared and longed for. How could it ever live up to either of their memories of that night they shared? David had told her she was a wet noodle in bed. She didn't want to be that for Jonah. She wanted to be the wild, passionate woman she'd been for him once. But how long could she maintain that facade? Was it better that she not try so hard and let him see the real Emma?

Jonah stopped in front of the bed and wrapped his arms around her waist. "Stop it," he chastised.

That snapped Emma out of her worried fog. "Stop what?"

"Stop overthinking it. Maybe that's all the tequila accomplished for you. It kept you out of your head, allowing you to just feel and go with the moment."

That may have been true. Emma found herself almost too nervous to move the more she thought about being with Jonah. She wasn't about to make love to a mysterious, heroic stranger. This was millionaire playboy Jonah Flynn. He was a man who'd romanced some of the most beautiful women in the world. She couldn't wrap her head around why he would want her. How could he not be disappointed with plain, boring old Emma? The thought was paralyzing.

Jonah seemed to notice the hesitation in her and compensated for it. His hands sought out the zipper on the side of her jumpsuit and pulled the tab to the end at her hip. "I guess I'll just have to overwhelm you with pleasure so you have no choice but to stop thinking."

His words coincided with his fingertips brushing along the sensitive bare skin of her side, making Emma gasp. He gripped the fabric at her shoulders and pulled it down. The silky material slipped over her arms, exposing her satin strapless bra, and then the slightly rounding curve of her pregnant stomach.

Emma instantly felt self-conscious about it. She had always been relatively slim, but never had the hard abs of someone who worked out at the gym doing core exercises. Jonah had seen her stomach when he was spying on her at the gym, but this was different.

He seemed to realize it, too. When he pushed the fabric of the jumpsuit over the curve of her hips, his eyes seemed fixated on her midsection. Jonah dropped down onto one knee, helping her step out of the outfit and slip out of her heels. Even then his eyes never flicked away.

When she was wearing nothing more than the bra and matching satin thong that wouldn't show through her jumpsuit, Jonah gripped her hips and pulled her to him. It reminded her of that first night where he'd done the same thing in his kitchen, looking up at her through his mask.

This time, as he leaned in to unfasten her bra and cast it to the floor, he pressed a kiss against the swell of her stomach. The gesture was simple and sweet, so unlike the man she envisioned from the newspapers. Emma closed her eyes to hide the glimmer of tears that started to gather there. Despite her worries and fears of Jonah rejecting his child along with her, it seemed as though she'd judged him too harshly. He would be a good father. That was all she dared ask of him for now.

She felt her panties slide down her legs and was too anxious to open her eyes again. There she was, completely naked in a well-lit room for his inspection. Jonah didn't seem to mind what he saw. He continued with his work, letting his hands and lips roam from her inner ankles up to her thighs. He stopped when he reached the exposed skin where her panties had once been. With a gentle nudge, he knocked Emma off balance and she sprawled back onto the bed with a shout of surprise.

Emma's eyes flew open in time to see the exposed beams and ductwork overhead. Before she could sit up and yell at Jonah, she realized he was kneeling between her spread thighs. She bit anxiously at her bottom lip as she felt his hot breath against her exposed center.

"I never got to taste you," he said. "Do you know how much I've regretted that?"

She covered her face with her hands to keep him from seeing her bright red cheeks. A moment later she felt one hand close around her wrists, pulling them away. He pinned them to the bed and when she finally opened her eyes, he was hovering over her. His shirt was unbuttoned now, showing off his lean, muscled torso.

"Does it embarrass you when I say things like that?" he asked.

Emma could only nod. How else could she explain that she was twenty-seven but about as comfortable with sexual topics as a twelve-year-old? She liked sex. And she'd had a good bit of it. But talking about it so blatantly? She just couldn't take it.

"Well, then I'll stop *talking* about it," he said, releasing her hands.

Before she could breathe a sigh of relief, she realized what he meant by that. He slipped down off the edge of the bed and pressed his palms against the inside of her knees to spread her legs wider.

The first touch was light, like a flicker over her skin that set off sparks under her eyelids. Every muscle in her body tensed in anticipation of the second contact. This time, his tongue lingered, moving slowly across her skin and making Emma squirm. After that, she lost count. Her hands gripped at the comforter as his lips, teeth and tongue feasted on her without showing signs of letting up.

Emma had done this before, and yet, she felt as though this were a totally new experience. Nothing any man had ever done to her had felt this amazing. She couldn't think, not really. Not when the waves of pleasure were coming at her from all sides. The only clear realization she had was that perhaps her lack of enthusiasm in bed with other partners was more of a reflection on them than on her.

It was as though a burden was lifted from her shoulders. Yes, perhaps David was just crappy in the sack and she accepted that because he was the kind of man she should want on paper. Successful, respectable, boring… The fears of becoming her sister had sent her on a path of living half a life. What else had she missed out on?

Emma looked up at Jonah and realized that he could definitely be the one to show her what was missing from her life. It might not ever be love or marriage or romance, but it would certainly be something more exciting than what she'd had. With a baby on the way, she had years of 2:00 a.m. feedings and runny noses in her future. She was excited to start that new part of her life, but there was no reason why she couldn't relish every second with Jonah now.

The thought released the last of the barricades she'd put up in her mind and she finally was able to relax and thoroughly enjoy the pleasure Jonah was giving her. She'd been holding tight to the release that was building up, somehow afraid to give in to it until now. When he slipped a finger inside of her and flicked his tongue over her swollen flesh, she couldn't hold back any longer.

Arching her back, Emma cried out. Her whole body convulsed against her will as the pulsating pleasure radiated through her. She clutched hopelessly at the blankets as Jonah continued his assault on her body, but there was nothing to hold her down.

This wasn't a release like she'd had before. Not even like the one he'd coaxed out of her the night of the Mardi Gras party. This blew them all out of the water and she found she couldn't control her body while it was happening. Only once the sensations finally faded away was she able to take a deep breath and lick her parched lips. She drew her legs together and melted into the bed like butter on a warm biscuit.

"That's my butterfly," he soothed as he stood up with a pleased smile curling his lips.

Emma could only watch him, the energy completely drained from her body, as he slipped out of his shirt, then went to work removing the rest of his clothes. Watching him was enough for now. There was so much of him she hadn't seen. He was lean and hard with the build of a marathon runner. Were there more tattoos he kept hidden beneath his clothes? In addition to their shared tattoo, she'd seen one peeking out from the sleeve of his T-shirts, but nothing she'd been able to study closely. Even now, she didn't really have the mental capacity to focus too much. Her body and her mind were gelatin.

"You seemed to enjoy that," he said. Completely nude, he offered his hand to help her sit up on the edge of the bed. "I'm anxious to hear you make those sounds again."

"Again?" she said, bewildered. She pushed herself back until she was centered, closer to the headboard.

Jonah crawled across the mattress until his body was covering hers. "Maybe even three times," he teased, pressing a kiss to her lips.

Emma couldn't imagine, but she wasn't about to argue with him while he was hovering between her thighs. With his lips still locked on hers, he pressed his hips forward, slipping inside of her with little resistance.

Now this, Emma remembered. She could hardly forget. He had been the perfect size for her, filling and stretching her body without being overwhelming. She drew her legs up to wrap around his hips and give him a better angle to go even deeper. The movement forced Jonah to pull away from her lips and curse softly with his cheek against hers. After a moment, he pushed up onto his arms with tightly closed eyes and a clenched jaw to maintain control.

"I don't know how you do this to me," he said as he withdrew and surged forward a second time. "It's like your body was just made for me.

Everything about you…your scent, your taste, the way you feel wrapped around me…I've been obsessed with experiencing this moment again. I can't believe I finally found you."

Emma couldn't believe they found each other, either. Or that despite everything, they'd ended up back in this place. She wanted to savor every moment they spent together so later she could use these memories to keep her warm on lonely nights. She reached up and cupped his face in her hands. The stubble of his beard was rough against her palms. She looked into his eyes, those blue, mesmerizing eyes, and drew his face down to hers so she could kiss him again.

"Stop talking and make love to me," she whispered against his lips.

Jonah grinned and kissed her full and hard before focusing on the task at hand. Adjusting his positioning, he settled into a slow, steady pace guaranteed to make them both crazy before too long. Resting on his elbow, he was able to dip his head down to nibble at her throat and taste her breasts, drawing hard on them until she arched her back and cried out.

He quickly adjusted his pace after that. They both knew that neither of them were patient enough to drag this pleasure on for too long. Jonah lifted her leg and hooked her knee over his shoulder. As he increased his speed and depth, Emma could only press her hands against the headboard to keep steady. That only made the thrusts more intense.

She couldn't imagine she could come again after the orgasm he'd just given her, but she felt the buildup start in her belly. She tensed her muscles and bit at her bottom lip as the pressure increased. She whispered soft encouragements between harsh gasps and groans as she got closer and closer.

"Oh Emma," he growled, planting a rough kiss against her inner knee.

Hearing her name on his lips was enough for her. She wasn't his butterfly, or his anonymous lover anymore. She was Emma. The one he wanted. And she came undone with her name on his lips.

As Emma cried and bucked her hips beneath him, Jonah finally gave in to his own pleasure.

With a loud groan, he thrust hard and poured into her.

With his arms quivering, he kissed her, and then rolled to her side and collapsed back against the mattress. There was a long period of silence filled by ragged breathing and the occasional sigh of contentment.

Emma was wondering if he'd expect her to make her exit soon, when he rolled onto his side and tugged her body against him. She snuggled into the comfortable nook he created for her and felt herself start to drift off to sleep.

When she was on the edge of unconsciousness, she heard Jonah's voice whisper into her ear.

"I know you think that we're not good together and can't be a family. I'm here to tell you, Emma, that I worked too hard to find you and get you back in my bed again. I may not be willing to let you go this time."

Nine

Jonah was awakened the next morning by his cell phone ringing. He untangled from his grip on Emma's naked body and rolled over to grab his phone from the nightstand. It was Paul, his financial advisor. With everything else going on in his life lately, it was easy to ignore the fact that he was trying to cover up his brother's embezzlement.

"Hello?"

"It's done!" Paul said, triumphantly. "The money is in your accounts so you can move it wherever you need to."

Perfect. Of course, now he had to do that with

Emma's eagle eyes watching the books, but what was done, was done. If he had to explain it to her, he would. He just didn't want to until the money was back where it belonged.

"Thanks, Paul. How much did it cost me to liquidate that quickly?"

"Er…" Paul stalled. "Perhaps a conversation better suited to a weekday at my office where we can look at all the figures."

That meant he'd taken a huge loss. "I'll be sure to take it, plus interest, out of Noah's hide."

"And we can hopefully make some of it back when we reinvest the funds."

Ever the optimist. "Okay. Thanks again, Paul." Jonah hung up the phone and scowled at the black screen. His advisor was working under the presumption that Noah was going to pay him back. He didn't have as much faith in his brother. Their mother would argue that he always treated Noah unfairly. Jonah would say the same of her. She coddled him, turning him into the monster that the rest of the family had to cope with.

"Is everything okay?"

Emma's voice drew him back to the here and now. "Yes, that was nothing. Just business."

"It's awful early on a Sunday morning for business." Emma yawned and curled into a ball against his chest.

Jonah wrapped his arms around her and clenched his jaw to hold in the angry words that had nothing to do with her. "Luckily we can go back to sleep," he said instead.

At first, his worry had been that Noah would screw up the Game Town deal. Covering up the stolen money had been at the forefront of his mind until he realized who Emma was. Then he'd nearly forgotten about why he was pursuing her in the first place. Now everything was different. Emma was more than an auditor; she was the mother of his child. She was the one who had held his interest, the one he couldn't forget about, the one who could make his blood race with a simple touch. It was possible that she could be The One.

How would she feel about what was going on with Noah? If she uncovered the truth, would she question every moment they'd spent together?

Could she trust Jonah knowing he had been lying to her about this the whole time?

Jonah might very well lose the Game Town deal because of Noah, but if he lost Emma... He would never forgive his brother for screwing this up for him. This was the closest thing to love he'd ever experienced before and he didn't want it ruined by another one of Noah's wild ideas before it even had a chance.

"What are you thinking about?" she asked softly.

"Nothing important. Why?"

She placed her palm against his bare chest. "Your heart is pounding like mad. I was thinking you were upset about something."

He wasn't going to ruin this moment with Noah's nonsense. If he had to tell her, he would do it later. "Did it ever occur to you," he said, tugging her tight to his chest, "that I just woke up to a beautiful naked woman curled against me? That can make a man's heart pound pretty hard. As well as other things."

Emma's eyes widened, teasing him. "You mean you want to do it again?"

Was it teasing? He wasn't so sure now. "Emma, I would make love to you ten times a day if you could take it and we could get anything else done. Does that surprise you? I don't know how it could."

She pulled out of his grasp and sat up in bed, tugging the sheets to her chest. "A little. I mean…this is going to sound ridiculous. I'm just not used to all that. I went to Catholic school and got my sex education from nuns. I was raised to be more conservative. Not so conservative as to wait for marriage, obviously, but I've never really had the wild kind of nights you're probably used to."

"Were all the guys you dated just that boring?"

Emma frowned, a crease forming between her eyebrows. "Yes, in a way. But I suppose that was what I was looking for."

Now it was Jonah's turn to sit up. "You were looking for someone boring?" He couldn't imagine someone like Emma wasting her life with someone like that.

"Not *boring*. More like…responsible. Respectable. The kind of man you'd be happy to take home to your parents."

"You mean the opposite of me?"

"No!" she insisted. "Well…not exactly."

Jonah tried not to be offended. He knew he wasn't the clean-cut lawyer or investment banker some parents wanted for their daughter. "Do your parents know you're having my baby?"

Emma shook her head. "They don't even know I'm pregnant yet."

"Emma! How could you keep that a secret?"

"Easy. I assure you that it was far simpler to avoid my parents than to tell them I'm pregnant but don't know who the father is. And I didn't until a week ago. Listen, my parents are very overprotective of me. My sister ended up being an embarrassment to the family. I was just a teenager when she died and my mother was constantly on me not to make the same mistakes Cynthia made. So I guess I've been more worried about pleasing them than pleasing myself. It wasn't until my ex said those horrible things that I gave myself permission to rebel for just one night."

"And look what happened!" Jonah said jokingly, but he could instantly tell by the pained expression on Emma's face that she felt exactly that way. He was used to scandal, but he sensed that Emma was out of her element with this entire situation. He opted to change his tactic. "Listen, I'm sorry about all this, Emma. I certainly didn't expect you to suffer permanent consequences from our night together. At least outside of the tattoo. I know how you feel—"

"How could you possibly?" she interrupted.

"Well, you might be surprised to know that my parents were very conservative and very strict. I wasn't allowed to do anything. Me and my younger brothers got sent to a boarding school in England when my father died. I only had a year or so left, then I returned for college. There, I realized that I could live my life the way I wanted to, and everything changed for me. I think my professional success is due in part to my rebellious management style. It doesn't work for everyone, but it really worked out for me."

"And what does your mother say about how you live your life?"

"She said plenty at first, when she thought I still cared. Then she realized I was a grown man, a CEO of my own company, and she finally let it go. At least until Thanksgiving rolls around. It wouldn't be a family holiday without Angelica Flynn putting her two cents in."

"I don't know that it will ever be that easy with my parents. Once they lost Cynthia, I was all they had left. I've never wanted to disappoint them."

Jonah put his arm around Emma's shoulders. "I don't know how you could possibly disappoint anyone."

Emma brought her hand to her stomach and rubbed the small bulge there unconsciously as she stared off across the expanse of his loft. "They won't be happy about the baby. My mother has been waiting years to put together a huge society wedding for me. Cynthia died before she could get married, so I'm her only chance to be the mother of the bride at an outrageous affair at The Plaza Hotel. You don't have a big affair like that when the bride is obviously pregnant. And there's no hope of a wedding at

The Plaza, or otherwise, when the baby is the result of a one-night stand and they have no intention of marrying."

There were a lot of things about Emma's pregnancy that he really hadn't taken into consideration until now. He'd only thought about how fatherhood would affect his life, not hers. Not really, and that was stupid and selfish of him. "Will your parents insist you get married?"

Emma shrugged. "They can try, but they can't force you into it. My father doesn't own a shotgun, so you're safe there. I'm certainly not going to force you into it. The pregnancy was a mistake. I'm not going to compound it by demanding that we add a marriage into the mix."

The last few days with Emma had changed a lot of the ways Jonah looked at the world. Once, long before she walked through the doors of FlynnSoft, Jonah told himself that if he ever found his butterfly, he wouldn't let her go. That hadn't entirely changed when he realized Emma was his fantasy woman. When he saw her, he saw a future without a line of women outside his door. Yes, he would absolutely stand up and be a father to their child, but for the first time in his life, Emma made him consider more—more than this cold, empty loft, trysts with random actresses and lonely nights working late at the office.

The idea of coming home after work to a nice, comfortable apartment and spending time with his very own family was suddenly more appealing than it had ever been. Having a family was something he'd never put much thought into, perhaps just because at heart he was still a teenager rebelling against his parents at every turn. As a grown man with a child on the way, things were different.

But it didn't sound like a future together held the same appeal for Emma. "You don't want to marry me?" he asked.

She turned to look at him with wide green eyes. "No, I don't."

Jonah had never asked a woman if she wanted to marry him before, and although it wasn't really a proposal, he was a little hurt by her blunt rejection. "Why? Am I not good enough to be your husband?"

"Of course you're good enough," she chided. "It has nothing to do with that. Despite the fact that we're having a child together, we hardly know each other, Jonah. *That's* why. We agreed to give the relationship time to develop and see what—if anything—happened, and I'm fine with that. If one day, you decide you're truly in love with me and want to marry me that will be completely different. But I'm not going to rush things because of an artificial ticking time bomb that ends with this kid entering the world. My mother and her dreams of a big Plaza wedding will have to just be dreams."

Emma had hoped that the weekend would clear her mind and she could return to work Monday ready to wrap up this project at FlynnSoft. Instead she found herself just as baffled by the discrepancy in the financials as she was the week before. If her calculations were correct, and she'd checked them three times, someone had taken out three million dollars without logging the expense properly. The money had been transferred to an offshore account she couldn't find any record of, nor did it have any relation to the corporation that she could find. It looked very fishy. And yet who would be foolish enough to steal such a large amount? Someone was bound to notice it.

This was the part of Emma's job that she didn't like. She had to tell the CEO that someone was stealing from him. Then she had to hope the finger didn't point back at Jonah himself. He had that right, she supposed—it was his company, after all—but it wouldn't look good. Then, worst of all, she had to report it back to Game Town, where the stodgy owner would likely pass on the contract. This wasn't going to end well for anyone but the creep who made off with three million.

With a heavy sigh, Emma picked up her phone to call Mark, one of her coworkers at the firm. She needed some advice on how to handle this so she could make certain she wasn't letting her relationship with Jonah cloud the issue. Mark had been doing this job for twenty years and had seen it all. He would know what to do.

"Hey there, Emma," Mark said as he answered. "How're the crazy kids over there at FlynnSoft?"

"It's definitely a different kind of company," Emma admitted. "Listen, I'm about to wrap up but I've come across something questionable that I wanted to run by you." She went through everything she found as briefly as she could. "Do you think I should speak to the CEO before I make my report?" she asked when she was done.

"You can. And I would. It's possible he can find an explanation and documentation for it that you haven't thought of. But if there's the slightest whisper of funds mismanagement, you need to report it back to Game Town. It's not your job to protect FlynnSoft from themselves."

Emma's stomach sank. "Of course. I just wanted a second opinion. Thanks for your time, Mark."

She hung up the phone and gathered some of her papers to take upstairs to Jonah's office. She hadn't seen him yet this morning. She tried not to think about what that meant. He'd said a lot about a potential future for the two of them, but she didn't believe it. Not really. It sounded good; it was the right thing to say, but would he follow through? Or would he chase the next shiny thing that caught his eye?

His secretary, Pam, wasn't at her desk when she came upstairs, so Emma went ahead and knocked on his door.

"Come in," she heard him yell from inside.

Emma pushed the heavy door open and slipped into his office. The moment he laid eyes on her, his eyes brightened and he smiled. Jonah leaped up from his seat behind his desk and rushed over to her. Before she could stop him, he swept her up in his arms and pulled her into a passionate good-morning kiss.

Emma tried to untangle herself as delicately as she could. "Jonah, please," she fussed, straightening up her paperwork and taking a step back.

"No one can see into my office, butterfly."

"Don't call me that at work, Jonah. And someone could walk in and catch us together at any time."

Jonah frowned and leaned back against his

desk. "I guess. But what if you worked here?" he asked. "Would you still worry all the time?"

"What do you mean?" she asked.

"Well," he explained, "I told you before that I need a new financial director. From everything I've seen of your work thus far, I think you'd be great for the job. And besides that, if you worked for me instead of this pesky third party, you wouldn't have to worry about the impropriety of it all."

It was a little more complicated than just that. She'd thought he was only joking when he'd mentioned the job last week. "No, I'd only have to worry about people saying I slept with the boss instead."

"Well, to be fair you did sleep with the boss," Jonah said with an impish grin. He leaned in and whispered "multiple times," like he was sharing a secret.

Emma shook her head. It seemed like everything was a joke to Jonah sometimes. "I'm serious."

"So am I," he countered. "I need a finance director and I want you to take the job."

"I'm not taking the job, Jonah. I don't like the way it would look."

"My brother works here. He collects a paycheck and doesn't do a damn thing. Everyone knows that and no one cares. Nepotism is alive and well in the corporate world."

"Yes, but if we continue to date, if everyone finds out I'm having your baby...I just don't like it. You know how I feel about that sort of thing. Reputations are important to me."

Jonah sighed. "Okay, fine. You won't kiss me. You don't want to work for me. I suppose that means you won't give yourself to me on the conference room table. So tell me what it is that brings you here today, Miss Dempsey."

Emma ignored his sexual comments and tried not to bristle at his sudden use of her formal name. A week ago she would've preferred it, but now things were different. Now she knew he was only doing it to get a rise out of her because he was irritated.

She clutched the paperwork tight to her chest and tried to focus on what she needed to say instead of the dark blue eyes that were watching her curiously. "I'm finished with my audit."

"Oh, excellent. You're very efficient, considering how much I distracted you. Does that mean you'll be free to be seen with me in public? Or do we have to wait for the Game Town deal to go through?"

"Well, the Game Town deal is what I came to talk to you about. I've found a significant discrepancy in the books."

The curiosity on his face instantly faded. His brow drew together with a serious expression of concern that seemed out of place on his face. "What did you find?"

Emma took the pages over to him where she'd highlighted the withdrawal. "Exactly three million has been taken out and wired to this offshore account in the Caymans. I haven't been able to figure out who it belongs to, but I can't make any connection to a legitimate business expense or account."

Jonah nodded, his face unusually blank of its usual emotion or amusement. His gaze simply flicked over the pages as she spoke without really seeming to take in the data. She wasn't sure what to think, so she continued to nervously prattle on.

"Do you know anything about this? I was hoping you might have some kind of insight that would keep it from looking as bad as it does right now."

Jonah turned his gaze to her and he nodded curtly. "I do have some insight, but unfortunately, it won't improve the circumstances. Please have a seat."

He returned to his desk chair and Emma lowered slowly into the guest seat where she'd first met the infamous Jonah Flynn a week ago. So much had changed and yet she was just as anxious talking to him now as she was then. "Am I missing something?" she asked. "Is this some kind of third world charity outreach in the Caribbean?"

Jonah shook his head. "I'm pretty sure we document our charity funds appropriately. You haven't missed anything, and I didn't think you would. The truth of the matter is that my younger brother Noah is a vice president here, as I mentioned earlier. He transferred the money out to one of his private accounts—an unauthorized loan of sorts. A member of the finance department brought it to my attention the day you arrived to conduct the audit. Had I known about it earlier, I would've disclosed the issue, but instead, I hoped that perhaps I could resolve it. I spoke with Noah last week and confirmed my suspicions."

Emma's stomach felt like the baby was flittering around with butterflies. Unauthorized loan? That was a nice way to say stealing. She'd never even met Jonah's brothers and now she was learning that one of them was a thief. Her *baby's uncle* was a thief. As though her parents weren't already going to have a meltdown over this.

"And?" she pressed.

"And, he's returning it all. I can't tell you what he needed the money for—I didn't ask—but he swore he would return it when he got back into the States. At the moment, he's in Southeast Asia. In the meantime, I have deposited enough money to cover the withdrawal. The accounts should register it as of this morning. Since this is a privately owned company with no board of directors to answer to, I've covered the loss and opted not to publicize the theft outside of the company."

"You still have the president of Game Town to answer to," Emma pointed out. "When I disclose this, I'm pretty sure Carl Bailey is going to back out of the partnership deal with FlynnSoft. He was suspicious enough of your company and its unorthodox methods going into it. I don't see him as the kind of man that would want to do business with a company that could potentially lose money it's handling on his behalf."

"We won't lose Game Town's money. I guarantee it."

"How can you do that?" she asked. Was he willing to use his own money to replace every dime his brother or anyone else decided they could take?

"I can guarantee it because I intend to make my brother's life so miserable he'd sooner stab himself in the eye with a butter knife than touch a penny of this company's funds again. When

I'm done making an example of him, neither he, nor anyone else in this company, would even consider it."

"Well, hopefully when you meet with Game Town, you can convince Carl of that. I'm not the one you need to sell it to."

"That's where you're wrong. I need you to understand that this is really a private matter between my brother and I, and I would like to keep it that way. I covered the loss and would do so again if necessary."

The unease returned. It all sounded very nice and good, but Emma couldn't shake the feeling that this was bad news. She believed Jonah and what he said about the money, but the implication was clear. "Are you asking me to leave the stolen money out of the report?"

Jonah looked her in the eye for a moment, as though he were silently pleading with her. But he didn't say the words. "I can show you the records of the deposits, Emma. Would that make you feel better?"

It would. To a point. "I would like to see those records. Then I can and will include in my report that the funds have been reinstated. But I won't be a party to covering this up. If someone were to find out, I would lose all credibility. I would be fired. I wouldn't be able to get a job anywhere in my field." Emma placed a hand protectively over her stomach, which seemed to grow a tiny bit every day now. "As it is, my impartiality will be questioned when the truth about the baby comes out. If anyone were to uncover that I knew about the theft and hid it…"

"You know you don't need to work, Emma. I can take care of you and our baby."

Emma shook her head adamantly. "Support your child because you want to and it's the right thing to do. I don't want it to feel like a kickback. Please don't ask me to do something that compromises my integrity, Jonah."

With a sigh, Jonah set aside the financial paperwork and walked over to her. She reluctantly let him wrap his arms around her and pull her into his protective embrace. "I won't. Report what you need to report, butterfly. FlynnSoft will recover, no matter what happens with the Game Town deal."

Emma eased back to look him in the eye and see that he really meant what he said. "You're okay with this?"

He nodded with a soft, reassuring smile. "I'm okay with this. In the end, it is what it is, right? You have to tell the truth and I have to be willing to stand in front of Carl and explain to him why he can still trust us to do a good job, despite it."

A sense of relief washed over her. She didn't like what she'd found, and she didn't like that Jonah and his employees might be punished for someone else's actions, but thankfully it would be out of her hands. "Thank you."

"When you get done typing that report up, I insist you let me take you out to dinner tonight. Anyplace on the island you want."

"I'm still not comfortable with us being seen together. It's not over until my report is filed, I'm back at my old office and the deal is done, Jonah."

"Okay, fine," he relented. "How about some very privately consumed takeout at your place, then?"

"Perfect," she agreed, letting him pull her tight

against him again. Even now, when it felt like things were unraveling, she was okay as long as she was in his arms. Hopefully she'd be able to stay there and weather the upcoming storms.

Ten

Jonah wasn't sure what to expect from Emma's apartment, but it wasn't what he got. Her work persona was so straitlaced and uptight, he anticipated her home would be boring, neat, with a place for everything and everything in its place. But the large and spacious apartment was flooded with daylight through large picture windows and the decor was relaxed, comfortable and filled with personality.

He followed her inside clutching a bag of Thai food from the restaurant up the block. Once he made it in far enough, he closed the door behind him and just stopped to take it all in. The fabrics on the curtains and the furniture were soft and romantic with florals and lace. The furniture itself looked comfortable like you would want to settle in and read for hours. It was soft, feminine with a touch of rustic country charm, telling him more about the real Emma than he expected to uncover.

"What's the matter?" Emma asked.

"Your apartment. It just wasn't what I was expecting." He followed her into the kitchen with its white Shaker cabinetry and gray-washed wood floors. A vase of multicolored zinnias sat in the middle of the kitchen table, likely from the flower shop on the corner.

"Not enough chrome and glass for your taste?" she asked. "Industrial chic isn't exactly my thing. I get enough concrete and steel walking around Manhattan every day. When I got my own place after college, I decided that I wanted something softer and more comforting to come home to."

"It's nice. Certainly more inviting than my place, but I'm more about function than anything. Here, I keep expecting a chicken to run across the hallway."

"You quit it," she chided, taking the bag away from him and unpacking cartons of Thai food onto the butcher-block countertop. "I don't have any pets, and that includes chickens. I think that's against the co-op restrictions," Emma added with a chuckle. "This is still the Upper East Side, you know."

They both made plates and bypassed the dining table to sit together in the living room on the couch. As they finished their food, Jonah found himself more curious about Emma's personal hideaway. He wanted to see it all and gain more insight into her.

"May I have the rest of the tour?" he asked as she set her mostly empty plate on the coffee table.

Emma shrugged. "If you want. There isn't much left to see. Two bedrooms, one bath." She got up and he followed her down a little hallway where she pointed out the black-and-white retro bathroom. "This," she said as she opened the opposite door, "used to be my office. I've cleared all that out to uh…for the nursery."

That was right. This wasn't just a cute bachelorette pad any longer. This was where she intended to raise their child. They stepped inside the room together. There wasn't anything in it yet.

"I thought it was too early to buy much. I had the walls painted a soft gray. I thought that was neutral enough for whatever I...*we* end up having."

"It's a pretty small room, Emma. The baby is going to outgrow it fairly quickly."

"I know," she said with a sigh. "I didn't buy this place expecting to raise a child in it. When the baby needs more space, I'll look at something larger. I want to save money while I can. If my parents haven't disowned me, perhaps they can help with a down payment."

It baffled Jonah how she continued to talk about the baby as though she was having to do this entirely on her own. "Or I could."

"Well...yes, maybe. I'm just not used to thinking about it that way. Up until a week ago, the baby's father was not in the picture. I had no idea how to find you, so I was having to make plans to do this all on my own."

"I may need a new place, too," Jonah said, thinking aloud. His loft didn't have any walls. How was a baby supposed to sleep without walls to block out noise? "Perhaps…perhaps we could look at getting something together."

Emma froze on her way out of the nursery. She looked at Jonah with wide eyes. "You want to move in together?"

"Uh…" When she said it that way, it was a little terrifying, but still accurate. "Yes. If we both need a bigger place, we could look into something large enough to accommodate all of us. Then the baby doesn't have to move back and forth between us. We could even look for something where you could have your own room, if that would make you more comfortable."

She took a ragged breath before pushing past him into the hallway. "That's something we could talk about," she said in a noncommittal tone he'd gotten used to with her. It was better than a complete dismissal. "We have time."

"Do you have a due date?"

"The doctor told me it would be November twenty-first."

With every detail, the baby became more and more real in his mind. Now he knew when to expect his life to change forever—before the holidays rolled around again. "A Thanksgiving baby?"

Emma nodded. "Seems like a long time from now, but it will probably be here before we know it." She continued down the hallway to the last door. "This is my bedroom."

They stepped into a room that was much larger than the nursery. A queen-size bed sat along one wall with a white wooden headboard that was worn and gouged to reveal the darker color of the wood beneath the paint. The bed had an eyelet coverlet and easily a dozen pillows, all different. An antique oval mirror, a dresser and an old cedar chest at the foot of the bed finished it off.

The place was nice, but the addition of a baby, plus a stroller, high chair, bassinet, toys and all the other accessories a child came with, would eat up the space she had left. It was a lovely, spacious apartment for a single woman, but that wasn't what she was anymore.

"We need to get a new place. This just seals

the deal. Your apartment is too small and mine is too impractical. I'm going to call a Realtor next week to have him start looking for apartments. How do you feel about the Village?"

Emma turned around to face him and placed a cautionary hand on his chest. "Slow down. I'm not ready yet, Jonah."

"Not ready to get an apartment or not ready for everyone to know we're together?" He asked the question knowing the answer. Emma and her blasted reputation. "When?" he pressed.

"Once the FlynnSoft deal is done. And we tell our parents. Then, if they haven't killed us, it should be okay to let others know about us and about the baby."

"It can't happen soon enough. I don't like hiding. I'm used to living my life out in the open. I can't wait until I can touch you whenever I want to. Kiss you whenever I want to."

Emma turned to him with a sigh. "It won't be too much longer. Until then, you'll just have to take advantage of your opportunities when they arise."

Jonah sat down on the edge of the bed and

looked at her. He had an opportunity right now he wasn't going to pass up. "Come here."

Emma took a few steps toward him, stopping when she was standing just between his knees. She placed her hands on his shoulders and looked down at him.

God, she was beautiful. The fact that she didn't think so just made her that much more attractive. Even when the mask had hidden most of her face, there was a beauty that shone out of her from the inside. Perhaps that was what he'd been drawn to all this time. No mask, no boxy suit, no stuffy demeanor could suppress it.

Jonah ran his palms along the outside of her legs, down and back up to her hips. There, he pulled her dress shirt out from where she'd tucked it into her waistband. He immediately sought out the silk of her skin beneath it, stroking her elegantly arched back and sides that seemed to quiver at his touch. She was content to let him explore, closing her eyes and just feeling him.

He unfastened her dress pants, sliding them over her hips to the floor. Once she'd stepped out of them, Jonah hooked his hand behind her knee and pulled her toward him. With little resistance, she crawled into his lap, straddling him on the bed. He ran his hands over her smooth thighs and hips before turning his attention to her blouse. One by one, he slipped the pearl buttons through the holes until Emma was astride him in little more than a lacy peach-colored bra and panties.

Emma reached up and pulled a few pins from her hair. With a shake of her head, the dark brown waves broke free of their restraints and tumbled down around her shoulders. The scent of her shampoo swirled around him. Jonah could only wrap his arms around her waist to hold her securely in his lap as he leaned in and buried his face in her creamy, lace-clad breasts.

She gasped and wove her fingers into his hair, pulling him closer as he teased and tasted her sensitive skin. His tongue rubbed across the rough lace that kept her nipples confined, over and over until the fabric was damp. Frustrated by the impediment, he tugged the straps down her shoulders until her breasts were exposed.

He kissed the inside of each one, then placed a kiss on the ridge of her sternum between them.

"Why are you wearing so much clothing while I'm wearing so little?" Emma asked. "I feel like I'm at a distinct disadvantage here."

"You're prettier naked than I am," Jonah replied with a grin. He immediately followed his words with action, tugging his shirt up and over his head. He wanted as much of his skin to touch hers as possible. He wrapped his arms around her and pressed his bare chest against hers before meeting her lips with a searing kiss.

He couldn't get enough of her. Not then and not now. She was unlike any other woman he'd ever known. She was his and he was hers in more ways than he could even describe. His butterfly had changed everything. And even if the thing with Game Town ended badly, he knew that if he made it out of this situation with Emma still in his arms, everything would be okay. She was his anchor, holding him steady so he wouldn't drift out to sea. He couldn't lose her.

Emma pulled away from his kiss, shifting in

his lap and grinding against his erection with a wicked grin lighting her face. "Now," she pouted.

He wasn't about to deny her. Emma rose up onto her knees while he scrambled out of his jeans and kicked them away. And then, she slowly lowered herself back down, taking in every inch of him at a deliciously slow pace.

"Oh Emma," he groaned into her hair, pulling her close as her heat enveloped him. "I'm never letting you go. Never."

She didn't want him to let go. She was content to stay right where she was forever. Emma had never felt so close, so connected to a man before. As she raised her hips and lowered them, rocking back and forth in his lap, the delicious friction her movement generated hit in all the right places.

A heat that started in her belly seemed to spread through her whole self. As her temperature shot up, the close proximity of their bodies made her skin break out in a thin sheen of perspiration. Each time Emma moved, her moist skin glided across his. Jonah only clutched her tighter as the sensations they were each experiencing grew more and more intense.

Emma wanted to find her release like this. She wanted to come apart wrapped in his arms. She wanted him to feel every tremble, every aftershock, and then she wanted to experience the same thing for him. This closeness was what she truly craved with Jonah. Here, in this moment, she could truly believe that they were supposed to be together. She could open her heart enough to let him in, if just for a moment.

She was roused from her thoughts by Jonah's encouraging whispers in her ear. "Ahh, yeah. That's my beautiful butterfly. Come apart for me, baby."

The low rumble of his voice against her ear and neck sent goose bumps through her body. She moved faster, rocking her hips hard until her muscles ached and her knees burned. It was when she almost had nothing more to give that she reached her goal. As suddenly as a snapping of fingers, her body gave in and the pleasurable sensations rushed through her.

Jonah held her tight, continuing to whisper to

her as her body shuddered and spasmed in his arms. When the rush subsided and she barely had the energy to hold on to him, he thrust hard from beneath her until with a final groan, lost himself in her. Jonah collapsed back onto the bed, taking Emma with him. After a moment, she rolled off and flattened into her mattress, drawing in a lungful of cooler air. They shifted around until Jonah could pull the covers up over them both and they snuggled together in the plush softness of her bed.

Lying there, looking up at her ceiling and listening to Jonah's heartbeat pound in his chest, she wondered if this could really be what her life would be like now. With the audit behind her, she would soon be free to be with Jonah. She wasn't sure how things would turn out, but even if they didn't marry, surely her parents would be happier about the pregnancy if they were together. If they *loved* each other.

Did she love him?

She had questioned her feelings for Jonah repeatedly over the last few days. Now, lying in his arms, making love to him again, it was easy to admit to herself that she did. She had loved him since that first night. She'd just been afraid to acknowledge the truth, even to herself. Love was a scary proposition, and love with a man like Jonah could be downright terrifying.

He was everything she thought she shouldn't want. Exciting, spontaneous, rebellious, passionate... For some reason, she'd lumped all those qualities in with irresponsible and dangerous, when that was hardly the case. She didn't need a man to be boring. She just needed him to be there for her. Jonah might very well be that man.

Emma was so content in his arms and so deep in thought that when her cell phone rang, she was tempted not to answer. And she wouldn't have except for the fact that it was her work ringtone. It was awfully late to be fielding calls from the office. Then again, they wouldn't call her if it wasn't necessary.

She answered the phone, seeing her boss's name on the screen. "Hello?"

"Emma. We have a problem," Tim said.

Her stomach instantly felt as though it had

twisted into a knot. How could they have a problem? She hadn't even filed the report yet. And she'd disclosed everything. She sat up in bed and grabbed her robe off the hook. "What's wrong?" she asked as she nervously walked out of the bedroom and tied her belt. She needed to focus and couldn't with Jonah's nude body sprawled on her bed.

"I spoke with Mark not too long ago. He told me about the conversation you had with him today. I really don't appreciate being left out of the loop on something so important. You should've come to me with this issue first."

Emma's free hand curled into a fist at her side. She went to her coworker for support and he'd ratted her out before she'd had a chance to do what she needed to do. "He gave me some advice and I'm following it. I'll have my report to you first thing in the morning. I wanted to read over it again before I submitted it."

"And what will the report say?"

"It will say that I discussed the issue with Jo— *Mr. Flynn* and he provided an explanation. Both the discrepancy and how FlynnSoft handled the issue will be included in the report for Mr. Bailey to handle as he pleases."

There was a long pause on the phone that Emma didn't like. When Tim was quiet, he was preparing his words, and they usually weren't good. "So you're on a first name basis with *Jonah*, are you, Emma?"

She swallowed hard, measuring her words carefully and trying to ignore the heat of Jonah's naked body that still warmed her. "The environment at FlynnSoft is very casual, sir. You know that as well as anyone."

"You know, Emma, I sent you because I thought you had some sense. More than Dee. I should've sent Mark, though. I underestimated Mr. Flynn's allure. I see that now."

Emma's mouth dropped open. "Sir, are you accusing me of some kind of wrongdoing? I assure you that my report is as accurate and impartial as Mark's would have been."

"So you're willing to sit there and deny any type of personal relationship with Mr. Flynn?"

Could she lie? No, she couldn't. But could she convince him it wouldn't matter? "No, I can't do that, sir. But I can say with complete confidence that I did my job as well as anyone."

Tim groaned loudly over the phone line. "Can't you see that he just used you, Emma? I'm willing to bet that he turned on the charm the minute you walked in the door. Did he offer to give you a personal tour of the building? Did he take you out to dinner and welcome you to the company? Just to be friendly, of course? He dates models and actresses, Emma. You're a pretty girl, but do you really think a man like him would be interested in a woman like you if he didn't want something from you? I'm pretty sure his entire plan from the beginning was to distract you from your work so you wouldn't find the problem in the books. Or if you did, to convince you not to disclose it. Now that it's done, he's going to drop you like a bad habit."

His sharp words hit their target, bruising her ego, but she wouldn't back down on her report. "But I *did* disclose it," she insisted. "I don't understand why you're saying all this when I haven't even submitted my report yet."

"Yes, you disclosed the problem, but then you

followed it up with the recommendation that the deal still go through because Jonah had handled it in a fiscally responsible manner."

"How…?" She hadn't submitted her report yet, and he'd just quoted her own words back to her.

"I pulled it off our server and read your draft when I got off the phone with Mark. I couldn't believe what I was reading. Would you have made that recommendation with anyone else, Emma? Tell me the truth."

Emma couldn't answer. She didn't know. Perhaps she wasn't as impartial as she thought. Perhaps Jonah had managed to get his way in the end without her even realizing he was doing it.

"You've lost your objectivity because you've gotten romantically involved with him, just as he'd planned. If I can't count on you to do your job, Emma, I have no choice but to let you go. Come in tomorrow and pack up your office."

She couldn't believe what she was hearing. It was everything she'd feared and dreaded since the moment she laid eyes on Jonah. She thought she'd been so cautious, so careful, and yet it was all falling down around her. "Are you serious? You're firing me?"

She heard the bed squeak and Jonah's heavy footsteps coming down the hallway. He must've heard her say she was fired. Panic started to close her throat. She couldn't deal with Tim and Jonah at the same time.

"I am," Tim said. "I'm sorry, Emma."

The line disconnected, leaving her dumbstruck. The phone slipped from her hand to the living room floor, where she left it.

Jonah appeared in the room wearing nothing but his boxers and jeans. "He fired you?" he asked, but she didn't answer.

She couldn't. Tim's words were swirling in her head and muffling Jonah's voice. She was pregnant and unemployed. She'd just lost her medical insurance. What was she going to do? Turn to her baby's father? The same man who may have very well used her to close the deal with Game Town?

That was the part that really ate at her insides. She wasn't the kind of woman Jonah was known to date. He'd pursued Emma from the moment he walked into his office and first laid eyes on her. Well before he knew who she really was, he was asking her to dinner, to coffee, buying her expensive flowers and pouring on the charm layers thick. Maybe Tim was right. All of this was just his way of securing the contract by any means necessary.

"Emma, what did he say? What's happened? Did he find out about us? We were so careful."

"Jonah, please," she said, holding out her hand to silence him. "Just answer one question for me. That's all I want to hear right now."

Jonah's jaw flexed as he held in his own questions and nodded. "Okay. What do you want to know?"

"Before you knew who I really was, why were you pursuing me so doggedly? The truth. Were you only feigning an interest in me in an attempt to distract me and keep me from finding that Noah stole all that money from the company?"

"Is that what Tim told you?" he asked.

"Just answer the question, please."

Jonah's blue eyes focused on her for a second

before they dropped to the floor. "Yes," he said after a prolonged and uncomfortable silence.

"Oh my God," she said, tears rushing to her eyes.

"Emma, no. Listen to me. Yes, that was my original intention, okay. I wanted to charm you a little to see if it would help things. I don't want to lie to you about that. But once I knew who you were, I was nothing but sincere. You're my butterfly. I—"

He reached out to her, but Emma dodged him. "Don't. Just don't. I can't have you touching me and calling me pet names when I'm trying to come to terms with the fact that you were just using me."

"Emma, please. You've got to listen to me."

"No, I don't. The only thing I have to do is pack my office tomorrow and update my résumé. I need medical insurance and a way to support my baby."

"Our baby," he corrected.

Emma only ignored him. She couldn't think about that right now. A future of dealing with him as her baby's father was too painful a thought. "I need you to get your things and go home, Jonah."

He took a step toward her, but she backed away and he stopped short. "I told you I'd never let you go and I meant it, Emma."

His eyes pleaded with her, the deep blue tugging at her heartstrings, but she didn't dare back down. He'd used her to get what he'd wanted and she couldn't forget that. He'd destroyed her career and her reputation just to save his own ass. "I'm not giving you the choice, Jonah. I need you to leave. Right now." Her voice was as stone cold and unemotional as she could make it with her feelings threatening to explode out of her.

This time, he didn't bother to argue. He returned to the bedroom, gathered up the rest of his clothes and pulled them on without another word. Emma followed him to the front door, fighting to hold in her tears until he was gone.

"I didn't mean to hurt you, Emma," he said before stepping out the front door.

She closed and locked it behind him, and

rested her forehead against the cold wood. The tears started flowing freely then.

"Well, you did," she whispered.

Eleven

"Someone is looking awfully grumpy this morning."

Jonah looked up from his desk to see his brother Noah standing in the doorway. Just the sight of him was enough to send his blood pressure rocketing.

His brother had chosen the wrong day to come strolling into his office with that smug grin on his face. He hadn't slept for days after the fight with Emma. He couldn't eat. The worst part was that he knew he'd handled the situation with her all wrong. He didn't know how he would fix things, if he even could. But he could get some justice by making the culprit that put him in that position pay.

Without responding, Jonah slowly stood up from his desk with his hands curled into fists at his sides. He had no doubt the waves of anger were rolling off him with the way the perpetual smirk on Noah's face faded.

Jonah stalked his brother around the room like a panther toying with his cornered prey. Slowly. Deliberately. Silently. He would savor this punishment. Weeks of frustration, heartache, not to mention millions of dollars—all because of his reckless, stupid younger brother.

"Jonah…" Noah held his hands up and backed away toward the conference room table. "Let me explain first, please."

"Oh, you're going to explain," Jonah said. "But you're going to do it with a split lip and a bloody nose."

"Oh, come on, Jonah. Physical violence? What would Mother say? I'm going to see her tonight. Do you want me to look like I've been in a fight?"

Normally, the mention of the grand dame

would've given him pause, but not today. "Nope," he replied. "I want you to look like you've lost a fight."

Now Noah looked worried. He moved until the conference table was between them. "Why are you so angry? Did the Game Town deal fall through?"

"Did the Game Town deal fall through?" Jonah said with a near-hysterical edge to his voice. He had no idea. He hadn't heard a word on the deal since he left Emma's apartment Monday night. He laughed and continued to circle the table. "That's the least of my worries at the moment, Noah."

That puzzled his younger brother. "Well, wait. Really. What has happened? Because I spoke with the Game Town CEO yesterday and he sounded like he understood and everything would go through just fine."

Jonah froze. He hadn't. Noah hadn't gone to their potential partner and spoken with him without even telling Jonah he was back in the country. He wouldn't. "You what?"

"I'll tell you everything if you sit down and

promise not to hit me. That's why I came here after all. I'm not stupid."

Jonah sincerely doubted that, but he was more curious about his brother's story at the moment. He couldn't fathom a scenario where he could explain the theft to Carl and have everything be okay. "Fine. But I still might hit you."

"Fine," Noah agreed. "Please sit down and let me finish first."

Jonah returned to his desk, his eyes never leaving his younger brother as he crossed the room and sat in his chair. Noah took a seat in the guest chair, perching on the edge as though he were preparing to make a quick getaway.

"Talk," Jonah demanded.

"I got back from Thailand two days ago," Noah explained. "The jet lag is unbelievable, really. I spent the first day in bed, and the next day Melody called me and told me there were whispers in the halls that the Game Town deal might not go through because of me and the money. I felt bad about the whole thing, so I went to Game Town and talked to the CEO myself."

Noah Flynn was not known for his initiative,

so Jonah refrained from interrupting him to see exactly what his angle was with all of this. There had to be an angle. Had to. Noah always had an angle.

"I explained to him what the money was for and that it was extenuating circumstances that would never happen again."

Every word out of his brother's mouth made Jonah angrier. "And what, exactly, was the money for, Noah?"

"Ransom."

Well, that was certainly not what he was expecting. Was he serious? "Ransom for whom?"

"For my son."

Jonah didn't think his younger brother could shock him any more than he already had, but Noah was always full of surprises. "What son? You don't have a son."

Noah sighed. "So, about a year and a half ago, I met this doctor named Reagan Hardy at a charity event. We spent a week or so together, but not long after that, she took her next Doctors Without Borders assignment in Southeast Asia. She found out she was pregnant after she left and never told me. Her high-profile work in the community made her a target of the *chao pho*, the Thai mafia. They kidnapped Kai from the clinic where she was working. I didn't know he even existed until she called and asked for help. They demanded three million dollars in seven days or they would kill Kai. If Reagan contacted the police or told anyone, they would kill Kai. I had to act quickly, so I took the money and got on a plane. I'm sorry it caused you trouble, but I'd do it again in a heartbeat."

Somehow, the knowledge that his infant nephew had been in the hands of dangerous criminals made everything else seem trivial. "What happened?"

"I paid the ransom, and they returned him unharmed. The cops picked the kidnappers up the next day and we recovered most of the money, so I have it to pay back, as I promised. When I told Carl about it, he was understanding. It's not the kind of thing that happens very often. He said that he wouldn't hold that against you under the circumstances. Did he change his mind?"

Jonah shook his head. "I don't know. I haven't

heard from Game Town. And at this point, I don't really care."

Noah studied Jonah for a moment with a curious look on his face. "The guy that nearly pummeled me a few minutes ago cared quite a bit. If you're not angry about the Game Town deal, what is it?"

Jonah didn't even know where to begin. How could he explain what he'd had with Emma and how he'd lost it?

"A woman has gotten to you," Noah stated.

Was it that obvious? "It hardly matters anymore, Noah. She was the auditor involved in this whole mess and she lost her job because of me."

"I'm sure you could help her find a new job. Hell, just hire her to work here."

Jonah shook his head. He knew Emma would say no, even now. Especially now. Everything blowing up in her face was just proof that she was right all along. "She wouldn't accept my help—I know it. Her reputation was the most important thing to her and I ended up ruining everything. Not just her job, but I screwed up us. She was the one, Noah. I love her. She's having my baby. And what did I do? I lied to her, trying to cover up the missing money and save our asses. It all blew up in my face."

"Is this the same woman from the Mardi Gras party? The one with the tattoo?"

Jonah could only nod. Just the mention of that night made the whole thing that much worse.

"Well, then you've got to fix it."

Jonah frowned. Things were always so simple to Noah for some reason. Even a harrowing kidnapping seemed to go smoothly for him. "How? I don't even know where to begin. I don't think she wants anything to do with me anymore."

"Probably not, but that doesn't mean it can't change. You said the most important thing to her was her reputation. So step up. Talk to her boss, tell them it wasn't her fault and get her job back. Taking the blame and making things right for her again is something you can offer her."

That all sounded good, but was it really enough? "What if she doesn't forgive me? Or does, but doesn't want me back?"

"Then you'll have to be content knowing you did the right thing."

For once, Jonah had to admit that Noah's idea was a good one. He might never win back her trust or her love, but he could make things right for her reputation and her career.

"Unless, of course, you're ready to make your big move."

Jonah's brows went up. "My big move?"

Noah held up his left hand and waggled his ring finger. "Give her everything she could possibly want from you in a two-pronged approach—restore her job and her reputation at work, and then restore her personal reputation and faith in you by declaring your love for her and asking for her hand in marriage. If she's that concerned about what people think of her at work, how does she feel about the fact that she's having your baby out of wedlock?"

"I already asked her to marry me. She said no."

"Well, ask again. And not because of the baby, but because you love her and you want to spend the rest of your life with her."

Once again, Noah was right. Jonah wouldn't say it out loud, though. Instead, he turned to his computer and looked up a few numbers. He had quite a few calls to make to put all this to rights.

"Who are you calling?" Noah asked as Jonah picked up his office phone.

"Everyone."

Emma was moping and she knew it. It had been a week since she'd been fired. At least she thought it was. She'd honestly lost track of time spent wallowing. She was pretty certain she'd worn the same cartoon-clad pajama pants three days in a row and hadn't washed her hair. She couldn't work up the enthusiasm to care. What did it matter? She had nowhere to go. No one to see. She was unemployed, single, pregnant and miserable.

Her phone rang just then, but she ignored it. She knew who it was just by the ringtone. Harper, Lucy and Violet all seemed to be taking turns checking in on her unsuccessfully. This time it happened to be Lucy calling. Emma had no doubt that before too long, they would show up at the door. They were on the visitor list and

Violet had a key, so there would be no putting them off in that scenario.

It didn't matter. It felt almost as though little did. At least for now. After a few more days, she'd have no choice but to pick herself up, dust herself off and move on with life. There were bills to pay and soon, a baby to feed. She could borrow money from her parents, she supposed, but that would require her to confess what a mess her life had become lately. She wasn't ready for that yet.

That meant she had to work.

Emma had been looking at jobs online. Her only hope was that perhaps she could find another position before word got out about why she'd left her last one. They would eventually call a reference and her company would disclose that she was terminated and ineligible for re-hire—she couldn't help that—but that would be better than the rumors that would build as they circulated. Especially once she could no longer hide her baby bump.

So far, she hadn't run across much of interest. There was a financial analyst position at Sandlin-Kline. That was probably a demotion, but she'd take it if they offered because they were a big firm where she could grow. They even had a day care for employees, which she would need before too long. There was also a CPA position at a large tax firm, which she could do, but it was a last resort. Taxes were not her favorite.

The only other job that had piqued her interest was the finance director at FlynnSoft. She'd giggled with hysteria when she saw the posting. Obviously she was a masochist for that to catch her eye. There was no other excuse as working with Jonah on a daily basis would be pure torture.

As it was, she would have to deal with him where the baby was concerned. Seeing him day in and day out, having him as her actual boss this time… That was out of the question. She was qualified for the position, and he'd already offered her the job twice, but that door had closed for them both when he lied to her. She would bag groceries at the corner market before she'd go crawling back to him for a job.

George and Pauline Dempsey would have

a stroke if they caught their pregnant, single daughter bagging fruits and vegetables. But she'd do it, because if nothing else, she still had her pride and she would work to support her child. At least once she got out of this funk and moved on.

Emma was pondering eating ice cream for dinner when her phone rang again. This time it was Tim's number. She frowned as she picked it up and studied the screen. Why would Tim be calling? Her last check was coming via direct deposit. She'd already cleaned out everything from the office. If he thought she'd be willing to answer questions about her accounts after he fired her, he would be sadly mistaken.

Unable to resist finding out what was behind the call, she broke down and answered. "Hello." She tried to hide the displeasure in her voice, but failed.

"Emma! Hey, this is Tim."

"I know."

"Do you have a second to chat?"

Emma sighed. "Not really, Tim. I've got an interview with Sandlin-Kline Financials first thing in the morning. I've got to pick up my suits from the cleaners before they close," she lied. She hadn't even submitted her résumé anywhere yet. She wasn't about to let Tim know that, though.

"Well, then I'll be brief, Emma. The truth of the matter is that I think I acted prematurely the other day in firing you. I was upset about being left out of the loop and I came down too hard. I shouldn't have let you go for that."

Emma slowly lowered herself down onto her living room sofa. Was Tim apologizing? Tim never apologized. There was something fishy about this. "I'm glad you recognize that," she said. She wasn't about to read any more into it, though. She hadn't known of a single person cut from the company that ever returned.

"Things have been pretty chaotic the last few days. I think I underestimated how much work you actually managed here. There's no way we can handle this workload without you. I know I've made a terrible mistake. I'd like you to come back, Emma."

Her jaw dropped silently as she tried to absorb

the information. He was giving her the chance to come back. "Are you serious?"

"I am. I really shouldn't have blamed you for Flynn's actions. There's no way you could've known what he was doing. He's a very charismatic and persuasive man. You did everything I'd asked you to do."

Emma paused. This didn't sound like the manager she knew. "Tim, did Jonah talk you into giving me my job back?"

There was a long silence on the line.

"Tim," she pressed. "Did Jonah Flynn call you and tell you to give me my job back?"

Tim sighed heavily. "He did. He came into the office in person this morning. He explained about the kidnapping and how the management at Game Town wasn't holding FlynnSoft accountable."

"Kidnapping?" Emma was suddenly very lost. "What kidnapping?"

"Flynn's nephew. That's what the three million was for. Did he not tell you that? Anyway, he said the whole situation was entirely his fault, that he pressured you into going along with it and that I was a damn fool if I let you go."

"A damn fool?" All she could do was repeat what Tim was saying because she couldn't grasp the conversation at all. Jonah's nephew was kidnapped? What nephew?

"Yes, that's a direct quote. And since I am not a damn fool, I decided I needed to call and ask you to come back. What do you say, Emma?"

She didn't know what to say. The fact that Jonah had gone to Tim and stood up for her was amazing. And unexpected. She hadn't heard a word from him since he left her apartment. After throwing him out like that she didn't really expect to hear from him until it was time for the baby to be born. He hadn't had to do this for her. And yet he had.

Perhaps he'd meant what he said that day.

Emma had been too upset in the moment to really listen to his protests. As far as she was concerned it was all just excuses to cover up the fact that he'd been caught. But if he'd really been sincere once he knew who she really was… If he really truly cared about her and their baby… He probably thought she wouldn't believe him, so he did what he could to at least undo the damage he'd caused.

Jonah knew this was important to her. But the job and her reputation suddenly weren't as important as they used to be. In that moment, they shifted to a distant second to the future of her family. Her future with Jonah.

"Emma?"

"What?" She realized she wasn't listening to her phone conversation like she should.

"Will you come back?" Tim repeated.

Emma thought about it for a few moments, but she already knew her answer. "No thank you, Tim. I appreciate the offer, but I think it's time for me to move on to other things. Good luck to you. Goodbye."

She hit the button, disconnecting the call before she could lose her nerve. And she did almost instantly. The second she dropped the phone on the couch beside her, she felt the panic well up inside of her. She'd just turned down her job. It frustrated her, but it was a good job. It paid well. What the hell was she thinking?

Was she thinking she didn't need it because Jonah loved her and wanted her back? If that was the case, she'd just taken a huge gamble. He may have only been trying to be nice. Or to put things to rights. And she'd tossed that gift back in his face. Now what was she going to do?

The chime of her doorbell drew her attention from her worries. What was the point of being in a building with a doorman when people could just trot up to her apartment unannounced? Who could it be, now? People just seemed unwilling to take the hint. She approached the door cautiously and peered out the peephole.

It was Lucy and Harper. As expected.

"What do you want?" Emma shouted through the closed door.

"What do we want?" Harper repeated. "It's Tuesday at seven, Em. What do you think we want?"

"I've called three times today, Emma," Lucy chimed in. "If you'd answer your phone this wouldn't be a surprise. It's girls' night!"

Shoot. Emma had totally and completely forgotten about girls' night. With a groan, she unlocked the door and pulled it open. "I'm sorry," she said. "I've lost track of the days, apparently."

Harper's appraising gaze ran over Emma's sloppy bun, oversize T-shirt and Eeyore pajama pants. "I can see that. Lucky for you, Lucy picked up everything for dinner tonight, so we won't starve."

Emma stepped back to let them in the apartment. "I don't know if I feel up to this tonight, you guys."

"Well, too bad," Lucy quipped. "Alice refuses to pay for cable despite her millions in the bank, so I don't get this channel at my place. I need to know what happens this week on our show. So I'm not leaving."

Lucy and Harper pushed past her and started setting up in her kitchen. Apparently this was happening whether she wanted it to or not.

"I'll go clean up a bit while you guys are getting dinner ready." Emma cruised through the living room, quickly snatching up tearstained tissues and empty snack cartons, and tossing them in the trash before she headed to the bathroom. She opted for a quick shower. By the time she emerged about fifteen minutes later, she felt a little more human and dinner was ready.

They gathered in the living room as they always did. This time, they each had plates of Greek food from a restaurant down the block from Lucy's place. Emma took a few big bites, savoring the first real food she'd eaten in days. It was so good it took her a moment to notice the other girls were looking at her with expectation on their faces.

"Where is Violet?" Emma asked, hoping to shift the discussion away from her for the moment.

"She's been MIA the last couple of days," Harper explained.

"I think she and Beau had another blowup," Lucy added. Violet had been dating an investment banker named Beau on and off for the last three years. "Who knows with those two? What's more important is what's going on with you and Jonah?" Lucy asked.

Emma told them about the phone call and how she'd just turned down the job offer from

Tim. Lucy looked as stunned as Emma felt, but Harper seemed pleased by her reckless decision.

"Good girl," Harper said. "Tim deserves to suffer for turning on you like that. I bet he's up to his ears in your work right now."

Emma wasn't quite as convinced. "You think it was the right thing to do? I wish I was that certain. I mean, what the hell am I going to do now? I've got to work."

Harper nodded with a wicked glint in her eyes that made Emma uneasy. "Of course you have to work. And I have the perfect job in mind for you."

Twelve

Jonah eyed the tiny Tiffany blue box on his desk. Today was the day. He'd made things right with Tim and hopefully Emma had gotten her job back. He'd talked to Carl Bailey at Game Town and Noah had been right—things were smoothed out there. All the broken pieces from the last week had been glued back together except for one.

Tonight, when Emma got home from work, he was going to her apartment. He would beg her forgiveness, swear his love for her and their baby, and then present her with the shiny two-and-a-half-karat Soleste emerald cut ring set in platinum that he'd picked up on Fifth Avenue yesterday evening. He would ask her to marry him—the Big Move as Noah had suggested—and hopefully, the last piece would fall into place.

Hell, he'd even worn a suit and a tie for the occasion. A classic, black Armani suit with a green silk tie that reminded him of her eyes. Every employee he passed in the hallway made a joke about him having a job interview somewhere today, as though he didn't own the place.

A soft knock at the door caught his attention. Jonah snapped the box closed and scooped it off the desk and into his pocket. "Come in," he replied.

Pam stuck her head into the room. "I've got the stack of résumés for your interviews today."

Jonah had forgotten about that. He'd agreed to interview a few candidates for the financial director position. His human resources team had already narrowed it down to the top three candidates for him to talk to today. Fine. Whatever. If they could keep his brother from stealing from him again, they were hired.

Pam carried the papers into his office and set them down on the blotter. "Today is the big day, isn't it?"

Jonah nodded. Pam always knew his business because she made his business possible. She'd called Tiffany's and set up a private, after-hours appointment to select a ring. She'd made sure a car picked him up on time so he didn't miss it. She was the one who saw to it that his suit went to the cleaners so he'd have it to wear today. She was pleased as punch to be part of such a big moment for her boss.

"She's going to love it," Pam insisted. "Don't be nervous."

"I'm not nervous," Jonah said with a smile, but Pam didn't seem to buy it.

"Of course you're not. You've just got to keep it together through a couple of interviews and you'll be fine. The first candidate should be here at ten."

Jonah looked down at his watch. He had about ten minutes. Just enough time to scan the résumé, finish his coffee and think up a couple of intelligent-sounding questions for the interview. He hated doing this kind of stuff. Hiring smart, capable people was his goal. It was also his goal to do so well at that, that the smart, capable people could handle hiring more smart, capable people without him.

This was a director-level position, though. After the minor scandal with Noah, he needed to be really cautious about who he chose to head up the finance department. He needed Carl and any other CEO who might want to work with FlynnSoft to be completely confident in their decision.

With a sigh of resignation, Jonah took a big sip of his coffee and picked up the first résumé. As his eyes scanned the top, the coffee spewed from his mouth, coating the paper in mocha speckles.

Emma Dempsey.

Jonah reached for a napkin and wiped up the coffee, dabbing her résumé carefully so he could still read it. Never in a million years did he expect her to actually apply for this job. He'd offered it to her more than once and she'd turned him down. Of course, now the Game

Town audit was over, maybe she felt freer to make that decision.

He tried to scan over her qualifications and education, but the only thought that kept running through his mind was that Emma was going to be here. In his office. In five minutes. He had her engagement ring in his pocket. Could he hold on to it for the entire interview and not give it to her? Play it cool?

Yeah, no. He was pretty certain he wouldn't make it through the meeting playing the coy interviewer and interviewee.

How was it that no one mentioned Emma applying before now? Someone had to have known. At the very least, Pam. Perhaps that was behind the twinkle in her eye earlier. He'd thought she was just excited about colluding over the engagement, but perhaps she knew something he didn't.

Another knock sounded at the door. It was exactly 10:00 a.m. and that meant she was here. "Come in," he repeated, and stood up at his desk.

Pam pushed the door open with a devious grin and behind her was Emma. At least it looked a bit like Emma, but not in any way he'd ever seen her at the office before. The stuffy suit and severe hair bun were gone. Her hair was down in loose brown waves around her face like it had been on their date. She was wearing a pair of dark denim skinny jeans with comfy-looking ballet flats and a T-shirt with a navy corduroy blazer over it.

It was the perfect mix of dress and casual, as though Emma had merged her style with his and finally found her niche here at FlynnSoft.

It looked good on her. Amazing. It made him want to reach out and stroke the waves of her hair between his fingertips. But he knew better. First and foremost, this was an interview and even if she had forgiven him, Emma would want to keep things professional.

"Jonah, this is your first applicant, Emma Dempsey." Pam grinned and disappeared from the office as quickly as she could manage.

He smiled and reached out his hand to greet her properly. "Hello, Miss Dempsey."

"Call me Emma, please," she said with a soft, knowing smile as she shook his hand.

It took everything he had for Jonah to let her

go, but he had to. "Please have a seat," he said, indicating the guest chair she'd sat in many times before.

Once they were settled, Jonah picked up her résumé and tried to think of something intelligent to say. He decided to continue as though they'd never met before and start with his basic opening question for any interview. "So. Emma, please tell me a little about why you want to work here at FlynnSoft."

Normally, this question would help him pinpoint whether or not the applicant had the same core values as most FlynnSoft employees. A love of gaming and graphic design, joy for their work, hell, even an interest in free coffee was worth a mention. People who appreciated his workplace innovations before they even started would be much happier and more productive employees later on.

"Well," Emma began, "I recently had an opportunity to work with some of the FlynnSoft family as part of an audit I conducted for my previous position. It was not at all what I was used to in a corporate environment, but after

I adjusted, I really learned to appreciate what FlynnSoft offers their employees."

"And what is that?"

"Freedom to work at their own pace on projects that excite them. All the tools they need— traditional or otherwise—to get their jobs done. Time and amenities to recharge and maintain their enthusiasm for their work. Also, an owner and CEO that truly cares for his staff. At first I thought he was all about the money, but I realized that so much of what motivated him was the success of his company for the benefit of the employees that depended on him."

"So you understand that despite how things might look, he was just trying to protect them?" he asked.

Emma nodded.

"And you realize that he would never deliberately hurt one of his employees, even if they were just on a temporary assignment?"

Emma looked at him with her big green eyes and he was happy to see no hurt hiding there. "Yes. I can see that now. At first, it was hard to believe, but I've had a little time to think about it and I've really come to appreciate what he was willing to do."

She understood why he did what he did. Jonah wanted to sigh loudly in relief and thank his lucky stars, but he wouldn't. Not yet. "Okay, great answer. Now, what skills and experience do you have that would be an asset to FlynnSoft if we were to bring you on board?"

At this question, Emma grinned. "Well, I am very structured and organized. I like to keep things professional in the workplace, but I also know when to let my hair down. I think that with my experience, I am the perfect candidate to keep not only the FlynnSoft financial department in line, but to keep the CEO himself in line, as well."

"Oh really?" Jonah's brows rose in curiosity. Now things were getting interesting.

"Yes. He has some weaknesses that I can exploit when necessary to keep things on track."

"What kind of weaknesses?" Jonah asked.

Emma's soft pink lips curled into a smile. "Me, for one thing. I happen to know that the CEO has a soft spot where I'm concerned."

Jonah leaned forward onto his elbows, getting as close to her as he could with the massive furniture between them. "That's true. You could probably negotiate an amazing benefits package with that kind of leverage."

"I'm mostly interested in maternity leave," Emma responded. "Flexible schedules and telecommuting are always good with little ones, as well. If my office was big enough, I would also like to be able to bring my daughter in to work with me."

Jonah opened his mouth to respond, but found there were no words. He had been following along until suddenly—*wham*! Did she just say *daughter*? They were having a girl? How could she know so soon?

Emma reached into her portfolio and slid a grainy black-and-white photo across the desk to him. He'd seen normal ultrasound pictures before, but this one had amazing detail.

"I had a 3-D ultrasound done yesterday. Fourteen weeks is still a little early to be absolutely sure, but the technician was very confident that I, we, are having a little girl."

* * *

Emma was fairly certain the interview was over. Jonah had managed to maintain as professional a face as he'd ever had, but the minute she slid the photo of his daughter across the desk to him, it was done.

Sitting there, she had the rare opportunity to actually watch a man fall in love with his child. It was something she thought she might never see before now, and she was so relieved she could almost cry. But she wouldn't. She could already see the sheen of tears in Jonah's eyes and the whole meeting would devolve into sobbing if she started.

Jonah stared at the picture for a few minutes before gently wiping at his eyes and setting it back down on his desk. "I am fairly certain we can accommodate whatever needs you may have to bring our daughter into the office. I'll kick Noah out of his office and turn it into a nursery if you want me to."

He smiled and stood up, walking slowly around his desk to her. He stopped just short of touching her, sitting down in the other guest chair beside her so they were at eye level. "I love you, Emma," he said without the slightest hesitation. "I love you and I've missed you so badly. I'm so sorry that I hurt you. I never meant to do that."

Emma reached out and covered his hand with her own. She gave it a gentle squeeze, reveling in the touch of his skin against hers once again. "I know. I love you, too. And I'm sorry, as well."

Jonah frowned at her. "Sorry for what? You didn't do anything wrong."

"Yes, I did," she insisted. Emma had put a lot of thought into this the last few days and she wanted to make sure he knew how she felt now. "I let my worries about what other people think of me interfere with living my life and loving you the way I wanted to. I've spent my whole life more concerned with what other people thought than what I thought of myself. I didn't like the uptight, boring woman I'd become, but I thought that's who I should be.

"You loved the parts of me that I was ashamed of, and it helped me to realize that what other people think of me is none of my business. All that really matters is that I'm happy and living my life the way I want to live it. And I want to live it with you. I want to make a family with you, Jonah, however we decide to have it."

Emma didn't care if they got married with a big Plaza wedding, eloped at the courthouse or didn't get married at all. The big wedding was her mother's dream anyway, not hers. A wedding and a marriage was only important if they put importance on it. All Emma wanted was Jonah in her life, and in her baby's life, every day. She wanted to love him and be with him. That was what would make her happy.

Jonah looked at her for a moment and she could swear there was a flicker of nervousness across his face. Before she could say anything else, he reached into his coat pocket and slipped out of his chair onto one knee.

He kept a tight grip on her left hand as he moved, so Emma had to clutch the arm of the chair with her right. Her entire body tensed up as she watched him and realized what he was doing. "Jonah…" she gasped, but he ignored her.

In his left hand, he held a Tiffany blue jewelry box. Before he opened it, he looked at her and said, "I know you said you didn't want to marry me the last time I mentioned it. You said we hardly knew each other and that if, given time, I fell in love with you and wanted to get married, you would reconsider." His thumb anxiously stroked the back of her hand as he spoke, making it hard for her to focus on his words.

Finally, he let go long enough to pull the black jewelry box out of its bright blue container and pry open the lid. He held the ring up for her to see it. Nestled in the velvet was the ring of her dreams. Emerald cut, surrounded in tiny diamonds and with a delicate band inset with even more. It picked up the morning sunlight in Jonah's office, displaying a dazzling show of rainbow colors. It was simply breathtaking.

"I'm hoping that you've reconsidered, Emma. I know that not much time has really passed, but this week without you has felt like a lifetime. I couldn't let another day, much less another week, go by without telling you how much I love you. And that I want to make you my wife." Jonah paused for a second to look her in the eye and swallow hard. "Will you marry me, Emma?"

How had she gotten to this point in her life? From her lowest moment before that Mardi Gras party, to the thrill of romance with a stranger, to the crushing loss of everything she held dear… And now love. Marriage. A family.

"I will. Of course I will, Jonah," Emma managed with tears filling her eyes.

With a cheer of satisfaction, Jonah leaned in and gave her a firm, soft kiss. Emma held his scruffy face with both hands to keep him close for as long as possible, but eventually he pulled away. Taking her hand in his, he plucked the ring out of its velvet bed and slid it onto her finger. It was perhaps half a size too big, but with her blooming pregnancy, she had no doubt it would be snug before too long.

Emma admired the glittering stone on her finger, then turned her attention back to her fiancé. "Thank you, Jonah," she said. "You're amazing and I'm so lucky to have found you."

Jonah stood up and shook his head. He pulled Emma to her feet, then wrapped his arms around her waist. "I'm the lucky one, butterfly."

They would have to agree to disagree. Emma

put an end to the discussion by pressing her lips to his and losing herself in his kiss. Somehow, despite the odds being against her, everything had come together and she couldn't be happier. Sometimes the scary decisions in life reaped the greatest rewards, and today, her reward was marrying the most amazing man she'd ever met.

A chime sounded over their shoulder from Jonah's computer. "Crap," he groaned as he broke away from her kiss and looked down at his watch.

Emma frowned at Jonah. "What's the matter?"

"Well, to be honest," he said with a sigh, "none of this was supposed to happen until tonight at your apartment. I wasn't expecting to see you this morning until I saw your résumé."

Emma wouldn't tell him that she'd sworn everyone, from HR to Pam, to absolute secrecy about the interview. "So?"

"So, you were my first interview of the day. I've got two more lined up after this. Why didn't they schedule you last? I want to take you home and make love to my fiancée."

Emma laughed, pulling back from his snug

grip on her body. "Well, that's not going to happen right now, so you'd better get prepared, Mr. Flynn. Even if you marry me, you'll still need a financial director."

Jonah narrowed his blue gaze at her in surprise. "You mean you don't want the job?"

"Of course I want the job!" Emma said. "But I want it fair and square. I told you before, I'm not letting anyone say I earned it on my back."

At that, Jonah laughed. "You're seriously going to make me interview all those people even though I have every intention of hiring you in the end?"

"Yes. I'm pretty sure your HR director would say the same thing. And if you hire me," she said, poking him in the chest with her finger, "it better be because I'm the most qualified." She might be marrying the boss, but Emma still had her pride. She'd worked hard to achieve a director-level position and she wanted it on merit alone.

Jonah studied her face for a moment and nodded. He took a step back and sucked in a deep lungful of air. Then he held his hand out to

Emma. "Well, thank you for coming in today, Emma. Pam will see you back down to Human Resources. I'm sure they have some paperwork for you to fill out and they can answer any questions you have about the company and our total compensation package."

Emma grinned as she shook his hand and picked up her leather portfolio. "Thank you for your time, Mr. Flynn. When should I expect to hear back from you about the position?"

With her hand still in his, he leaned in and whispered into her ear. "I'll be at your place by six."

* * * * *

MILLS & BOON®
Large Print – November 2017

ROMANCE

The Pregnant Kavakos Bride	Sharon Kendrick
The Billionaire's Secret Princess	Caitlin Crews
Sicilian's Baby of Shame	Carol Marinelli
The Secret Kept from the Greek	Susan Stephens
A Ring to Secure His Crown	Kim Lawrence
Wedding Night with Her Enemy	Melanie Milburne
Salazar's One-Night Heir	Jennifer Hayward
The Mysterious Italian Houseguest	Scarlet Wilson
Bound to Her Greek Billionaire	Rebecca Winters
Their Baby Surprise	Katrina Cudmore
The Marriage of Inconvenience	Nina Singh

HISTORICAL

Ruined by the Reckless Viscount	Sophia James
Cinderella and the Duke	Janice Preston
A Warriner to Rescue Her	Virginia Heath
Forbidden Night with the Warrior	Michelle Willingham
The Foundling Bride	Helen Dickson

MEDICAL

Mummy, Nurse...Duchess?	Kate Hardy
Falling for the Foster Mum	Karin Baine
The Doctor and the Princess	Scarlet Wilson
Miracle for the Neurosurgeon	Lynne Marshall
English Rose for the Sicilian Doc	Annie Claydon
Engaged to the Doctor Sheikh	Meredith Webber

1017 GEN STD LP

MILLS & BOON®
Hardback – December 2017

ROMANCE

His Queen by Desert Decree	Lynne Graham
A Christmas Bride for the King	Abby Green
Captive for the Sheikh's Pleasure	Carol Marinelli
Legacy of His Revenge	Cathy Williams
A Night of Royal Consequences	Susan Stephens
Carrying His Scandalous Heir	Julia James
Christmas at the Tycoon's Command	Jennifer Hayward
Innocent in the Billionaire's Bed	Clare Connelly
Snowed in with the Reluctant Tycoon	Nina Singh
The Magnate's Holiday Proposal	Rebecca Winters
The Billionaire's Christmas Baby	Marion Lennox
Christmas Bride for the Boss	Kate Hardy
Christmas with the Best Man	Susan Carlisle
Navy Doc on Her Christmas List	Amy Ruttan
Christmas Bride for the Sheikh	Carol Marinelli
Her Knight Under the Mistletoe	Annie O'Neil
The Nurse's Special Delivery	Louisa George
Her New Year Baby Surprise	Sue MacKay
His Secret Son	Brenda Jackson
Best Man Under the Mistletoe	Jules Bennett

MILLS & BOON®
Large Print – November 2017

ROMANCE

An Heir Made in the Marriage Bed	Anne Mather
The Prince's Stolen Virgin	Maisey Yates
Protecting His Defiant Innocent	Michelle Smart
Pregnant at Acosta's Demand	Maya Blake
The Secret He Must Claim	Chantelle Shaw
Carrying the Spaniard's Child	Jennie Lucas
A Ring for the Greek's Baby	Melanie Milburne
The Runaway Bride and the Billionaire	Kate Hardy
The Boss's Fake Fiancée	Susan Meier
The Millionaire's Redemption	Therese Beharrie
Captivated by the Enigmatic Tycoon	Bella Bucannon

HISTORICAL

Marrying His Cinderella Countess	Louise Allen
A Ring for the Pregnant Debutante	Laura Martin
The Governess Heiress	Elizabeth Beacon
The Warrior's Damsel in Distress	Meriel Fuller
The Knight's Scarred Maiden	Nicole Locke

MEDICAL

Healing the Sheikh's Heart	Annie O'Neil
A Life-Saving Reunion	Alison Roberts
The Surgeon's Cinderella	Susan Carlisle
Saved by Doctor Dreamy	Dianne Drake
Pregnant with the Boss's Baby	Sue MacKay
Reunited with His Runaway Doc	Lucy Clark

1117 GEN STD LP